Playing Jasper

Genoa Mafia Series Book IV

By Ginger Ring

Playing Jasper

Limitless Publishing, LLC
Kailua, HI 96734
www.limitlesspublishing.com

Formatting: Limitless Publishing
Photographer: JW Photography
Model: Daniel Rengering

ISBN-13: 978-1-64034-618-5
ISBN-10: 1-64034-618-X

Prologue

Sid

"Check, please." Sid Messina waved at the waiter.

"This was a wonderful meal." His wife, Karen, pushed her dessert plate away and dabbed at her lips with the cloth napkin.

"Good. I'm so glad you enjoyed it." The man handed the server his card. "Because after tomorrow, we probably won't be able to show our faces in this part of town again."

"You really think it'll be that bad?" Her face had always been beautiful, but the stress of the last few months had added a line here and there. She'd worked as hard on the story as he had. Unfortunately, his name would be the only one listed. Despite his pleading, she'd insisted that he should get the glory, if they could call it that. When the headlines hit, it'd be a shitstorm.

1

"We may have to go into hiding." Sid took a sip of wine. His wife hadn't taken his last name, so they could go by that, if necessary.

"Here you go." The waiter set the small silver tray with their card and receipt on the table. "Enjoy the rest of your evening." The young man nodded and left.

Karen remained composed, but as soon as they were alone again, her smile vanished. "Do you really think so?"

"Dear, we're about to blow the lid off the biggest crime organization in the Midwest. This is huge. This will be as big as bringing Gotti down." He reached across the table and took her hand in his. "You knew that going in."

"I know, and I'm so proud of the work you've done, but now that it's about to become a reality," she touched her free hand to her heart, "I'm scared." Her confession broke his heart. She wasn't the only one that was worried. It'd started out as research on an anonymous tip, and things had spiraled from there.

"It'll be all right. The paper is fully behind me." At least his editor, Mr. Hower, was. Unfortunately, even he said to keep things quiet until they went to press. No one else knew but the three of them. Right before they'd left to go out to eat, Sid had pressed the SEND key. Mr. Hower was at the office right now, going over the copy word for word. The man had cleared several hours tonight to work on it and fine tune it to be published in tomorrow's paper.

Karen smiled and reached for her purse. "I'm glad our daughter's off at college. When this hits the stands, I've a feeling our lives will change forever, whether we want it to or not."

"Just look at it like this. When I get my first book deal, I'll buy you more of those high-priced handbags you love."

"I'd rather have you than a fancy bag any day of the week." They both rose, and she gave him a kiss. It wasn't a peck on the cheek, either. The kiss took him off guard. Almost like they were saying goodbye.

Even though the food was top notch, the delicious meal now sat in his stomach like a heavy rock. The weight of what they were about to do was almost too much to bear, but it had to be done. People's lives were at stake. He'd also put way too much time and effort into this exposé to drop it now. "Can't you just tell your boss you changed your mind?" Her head titled like a puppy dog, and she gave him that half-smile that he'd always loved. That usually caused him to cave, but he was sticking to his guns this time.

"You know I can't do that." It was too late. He'd lose his job if he did, and they had bills to pay. The tuition payments alone were killing them, but they'd never let on to their little girl. The damage was done anyway. In just the last week, the sinking feeling of someone following Sid had trailed him wherever he went. They'd need the income and notoriety the story would bring to keep them safe and above water.

"It was worth a try." Karen cupped his face in her hand. "I'm really proud of you, and I know our daughter is too. Let's go home, have a bottle of wine, and celebrate your future Pulitzer Prize-winning story."

"Ha. Now you're talking, but don't count your chickens before they hatch." He placed his hand on her lower back as they weaved their way through the tables to the exit. "But just in case, I might add more shelf room in the living room for my trophies and another shelf in the closet for all those handbags I'm going to buy you."

"You do that." She giggled as the host at the front of the restaurant opened the door and wished them a good night.

It was late September, but there was already a chill in the air. Sid buttoned his coat, and his wife tucked her hand in his elbow as they walked the short distance toward their car. The phone in his pocket buzzed, and he pulled it out. Sid's gaze met his wife's, and he smiled. It was their only child and the love of their lives.

"Hey, pumpkin. What's new?" They both stopped on the sidewalk.

"You know I'm in college. You can stop calling me different kinds of fruit." Just the sound of her voice warmed his heart.

They'd both loved puns, and it'd been a running joke between the two for years. "You know I can't do that. You're the apple of my eye."

"You're such a peach, Dad." He'd hit the speakerphone so her mom could hear.

"Hi, honey." The two looked so much alike. Thankfully. His daughter had inherited her mother's gorgeous red hair and not the thick black mess that topped his head. As far as he was concerned, the girl had been blessed with the best of both. Her mother's grace, looks, and strength and his height, ambition, and brown eyes. They were both so damn proud of her.

"What are you doing? I hear cars. Are you outside?" His daughter should've been a detective; she was more observant than anyone he knew.

"Yes, we were just at Alessio's. You'll have to come with us next time you're home."

"I'd love that. You know Italian is my favorite food." She got that from him also. Whereas his wife was Irish and Norwegian, he was full-blooded Italian. They were the two most important people in his life, and he'd die for either one of them.

"Are you dating anyone? Meet any nice boys yet?" Karen piped in. He rolled his eyes at his wife, and she just shrugged her shoulders.

"No, I don't have time for that. School is the main thing in my life right now." Her voice echoed on the phone.

"That's my girl." Sid chuckled. "Hey, we're almost to the—"

A car skidded to a stop in the street, and two men jumped out. The fact that they held guns registered too late for him to react. Rapid gunfire sounded, and pain like he'd never experienced ripped through his chest. Sid fell backward. Stunned. In a fog, he turned his head. Karen was on the ground beside him. Her pretty ivory dress was covered in red.

No, no, no, Sid mumbled, or was it just in his head? His heart pounded as he crawled to her side. Blood covered his hands, and the phone he clutched slipped the few inches to the ground. This couldn't be happening. The aching was so severe, he couldn't breathe. He coughed, and blood sprayed the cement.

"Dad? Mom? What's going on?" He reached for the phone but couldn't make it. Sid flopped around in agony. There was no doubt he was bleeding out and didn't have much time left in the world. He didn't have to be a doctor to know that. Sweat covered his face as he reached for his wife again, but it was no use. There was no strength left, and she was probably dead. A tear slipped down his cheek. This was his fault, even if he hadn't pulled the trigger himself. He'd caused this, and that hurt worse that any bullet ever could.

The men with the guns surrounded them and spoke in a foreign language. Both dressed in suits as if they'd been going to a late dinner as soon as the job was done. He didn't recognize any of them, but it was a good bet who they worked for. One young man stared down at his wife with a haunted look on his face. The other was solely focused on him.

His phone buzzed again, and it took everything he had to turn and read the screen. He didn't need to see it to know who it was. His pride and joy was calling back. As the leader of the group pointed a gun to Sid's head, the only thing that gave him peace was the fact that his daughter wasn't there.

Chapter One

Lake Genoa, Present Day

Jackie

The alarm wouldn't stop ringing, but she lacked the energy to turn it off. She was in a rut, and mornings were the worst. Most people spend a large part of their lives at work, and Jackie Smith just wasn't digging hers right now. Sure, no one really liked work. It's called work for that very reason. That said, there had to be more to life than this.

Living in a small town wasn't what she thought it'd be. It'd made her soft. The edge was gone. On one of those cold nights last winter, she'd felt daring and left her car running with the keys inside. The few minutes she spent in the grocery store while it sat idling had her blood flowing. Would it be there when she came out? It was a stupid thing to do, but she was bored.

When Jackie came out, the car was still there. As were all the other vehicles that were also running, the steam from their exhaust pipes keeping each other company. It would have been a story, something exciting to finally write about. She could see the headline now:

CAR STOLEN WHILE OWNER STOCKED UP BEFORE THE STORM.

Jackie knew she shouldn't complain about the lack of crime, but working for the paper, there were only so many sunny-side-up stories she could write. Nothing ever happened here, and it was wearing on her.

The paper struggled for sales, as did most, in the social media age. If things didn't pick up soon, she'd be out of a job and circling help wanted ads in the classified section. Being the last hired, Jackie would be the first out the door, and rumors were already circling in the break room. The paper ran with a skeleton crew, and if she got the boot, there'd be even more work for those left behind.

Unable to ignore the alarm any longer, Jackie dragged herself out of bed and stretched. Saying she was tired would be an understatement. Hell, maybe she was depressed, craving a boyfriend, a change of scenery, something?

The only thing she needed for certain right now was coffee and lots of it. Too much caffeine sometimes gave her heart palpitations, but she was young enough not to be too concerned with that. Today, it wasn't the occasional treat from the Genoa Java causing the heartache; it was the daily stuff at work that gave her issues. There was that W word again. Work. Work. Work. W.O.R.K.

Grabbing a fleece robe, she freshened up in the bathroom before hitting the fridge for some juice. With OJ in hand and a book in the other, Jackie settled into a chair on the balcony overlooking the lake. She really did love where she lived. The place was a steal. Low rent with a million-dollar view. Nothing to complain about there. She still couldn't believe her luck when this place came up for rent. There were some advantages of working at the Genoa Globe. In addition to writing stories, everyone who placed a classified ad had to go through her first.

The wealthy owner of the condo gave her an offer over the phone that she couldn't refuse. The only requirements were to keep an eye on the place, watch for riff raff, and call the numbers on the list if anything went wrong or broke. Jackie got the place for next to nothing. So far, everything was perfect and in great working order. The distance from the newspaper office was less than a mile. It was an easy walk, for sure, and one thing she really did enjoy.

Taking a sip of fresh juice, she opened the book that had been on her shelf for months. It was called *Contract from Hell* by local author Stephanie Barclay. The author's boyfriend, Dominic, had proposed marriage at the book signing. It was a romantic gesture from someone who looked like a cross between a hot lumberjack and an ax murderer.

Jackie was supposed to have an interview with the author, but that never came to light. For some reason, after the release party, Stephanie seemed to disappear from the lime light. There were rumors that the story she wrote was true. That she'd run from an arranged marriage with a Russian mobster who trafficked in women, and that certain high-ranking mafia figures, even though they were featured under their fake names, didn't wish for her to speak publicly. It was even suggested that her future husband fought a battle to the death to win her away from the bratva. It was an unbelievable story. Could it be true?

She'd not seen her since. Was Stephanie off the grid or just busy planning the wedding of her dreams? The woman had a website, but there were no photos of her face, just excerpts, teasers, and buy links. *Contract from Hell* had done amazing on the charts. There was even talk of a film option, but again, what would those criminal connections have to say about that?

If only she could've gotten an exclusive with Stephanie. That would have energized her career and removed the bad groove she was in. Career? What career? Maybe she wasn't meant to be a reporter. She wouldn't be the first one to not do what she'd gone to college for. Not the first one to change horses in mid-stream, as the saying goes.

Jackie skimmed the first chapter and glimpsed at the clock on the kitchen wall inside.

"Dang. I better get going!" She hurried inside to get dressed and put on some makeup. Grabbing a light jacket and her purse, Jackie rushed out the door. It was early May, by noon it would be warm enough to shed the extra layer, but for now, she was glad to have it.

Her open-toed ankle boots clicked on the sidewalk. The tour boats bobbed in the water as she passed. Soon the mailboat would be heading out to deliver the mail. It was a long-standing tradition in Lake Genoa. In the 1800s, most of the homes on the lake were summer homes and only accessible from the water. Their mail was delivered daily by boat. Mailboxes were located at the end of the private wooden docks. As the boat passed, a person would jump out of the front of boat, put the mail in the box, and jump back on the back of the boat, all while it was moving.

As Jackie strolled through downtown, the smell of the Java Shop enticed her to stop in. The place buzzed with early morning customers as she got in line. A couple of beautiful, well-dressed women stood in front of her. They looked familiar, but right now, fatigue didn't have her at her sharpest. The one holding a baby was sporting red-soled shoes that probably cost a fortune. Blessed with height as it was, Jackie had no use for high heels and would most likely fall on her face if she ever tried walking in heels like those. The woman's companion was also stunning. That lady paid for their five-dollar coffees with an Amex black card pulled from what looked like a several thousand-dollar purse.

Even though Genoa was a small town, it was one of the wealthiest communities in the state, maybe even the country. There wasn't a piece of real estate on the lake that paid less than one-hundred-thousand dollars a year in property taxes. She may not have been much of a reporter, but her attention to detail, when she wanted it, was spot on. Jackie

11

couldn't recall the pair's names, but she did know they were locals. It would come to her later, when she'd be in the middle of trying to remember something else.

"What can I get you, ma'am?" The young barista smiled. Jackie could deal with people calling her hon, sweetie, or miss, but ma'am bugged her to no end.

"I'll have the caramel mocha with vanilla." She paid the bill, waited for her drink, and headed out the door.

Three short blocks more and she'd reached the old brick building that was the home of the Genoa Globe.

"Hey, Jackie," a few co-workers called as she passed their desks. When she reached her writing table, she tossed her purse into a drawer and logged onto her computer. They were on a deadline. The paper came out on Tuesdays, so everything had to be entered, edited, and ready to go to print by four.

This was the busiest day, as all the scores from school games and local events from the weekend had to be added. They had an online edition, but it still needed to be uploaded for the paper edition. Yes, people still liked to buy the local paper, especially tourists that weren't signed up online. There was still something about opening a paper or smelling the pages of a paperback that would always be timeless.

The morning flew by as she worked on getting everything done.

"Excuse me," a woman called from the front counter, and Jackie looked up from her laptop. She rose from her desk and headed toward the front of the room.

"Hi, what can I help you with?" As she neared the customer, it dawned on her that this was one of the women she'd seen at the coffee shop. The one carrying the designer purse, not the baby.

"I'd like to put an ad in the paper." She dug in her high-end handbag, a Louis Vuitton if Jackie had to guess, and pulled out a piece of paper.

"What kind of an ad do you want to place?" Logging into the front desk computer, Jackie pulled up the screen with all the information for the classifieds.

"Help wanted." The woman slid the piece of paper toward her. "We purchased a winery outside of town and are looking for more staff for the summer."

"A winery?" Jackie glanced at the details on the paper. "That sounds like a dream job. I love wine."

"Well, you can't drink on the job, but we do offer great benefits and an opportunity to learn the business with us." The woman smiled. "You should stop in sometime. Here's my card." She handed her a business card. The name on the front proclaimed her as Madison Caponelli. It was a black card embossed with gold letters. Very classy.

"Thanks. I will." She tucked the card into her pants pocket. "So, it looks like we have all your details." Jackie turned the screen so Madison could see. "Here are the sizes and costs of the ads. Do you see one that you like?"

Her client pointed to the one she wanted. "This size would be great. Can we get it in tomorrow's paper?"

"I, ah…" Jackie glanced at the clock.

"Of course, we can, Mrs. Caponelli." Bruce, her boss, came out of nowhere. The guy buttoned his jacket and smoothed back his hair. Where'd he get a suit jacket? The Genoa Globe was anything but fancy.

"Bruce, please." Their client rolled her eyes. "I've known you all of my life. Cut the 'Mrs.' crap."

"Sorry. I didn't mean any disrespect." Bruce tugged at his collar. "Jackie will get right on it. We always have room for Caponelli business."

"And we appreciate it." Madison handed her a thick, black credit card, and she ran it through the card reader.

After it was processed, Jackie returned the card to her and picked up the paper with the job description on it. "I think we have everything we need. I'll get working on this right away."

"Thank you. I appreciate it." Madison gathered her purse and nodded to Bruce. "See you around."

"Yes, thanks, Madison. Have a good day." He waved and Jackie shook her head. What was wrong with the guy?

"You too." The woman smiled at both and left.

Jackie stared out the front window and noticed a large man open the door for her.

"Is that Mr. Caponelli?" she whispered to her boss as they watched them both leave the building.

"No, that's her bodyguard." Bruce exhaled.

"Bodyguard. Is she famous or something?" Curiosity kicked in and jolted her wide awake. She knew that name, everyone did, but it was important to get his take on the family.

"Madison's a local girl, but she married Roman Caponelli, the son of a major Chicago mafia don. After he moved here, things haven't been the same."

"How so?" He briefly filled her in on some of the higher points, but she'd be searching online as soon as she reached her desk.

"What's with the winery? That sounds like a pretty normal business for this area." Wisconsin was filled with vineyards.

"You'd think so, but I don't put anything past that guy. Madison's in love. She sees what she wants to see."

"Not me. I don't care if he's the hottest guy in the world; I'd never get involved with a criminal."

That's just nuts.

Jackie grabbed the paper and headed to her desk, but Bruce followed.

"You know what they say. Love is blind."

"Still not worth it." Jackie turned her head. "So, the winery?"

"I think the place is legit. It's in his wife's name, and she'd never allow anything illegal to go on there. He also wouldn't risk it."

Taking a seat, Jackie punched in the name of their winery. The wheels already turned in her head. The story was there; she could feel it. Her fingers tingled as they punched the keys.

"From the website, it looks normal. The vineyard has been around for years, and they just put it up for sale this spring." Reaching for a pencil, she tapped it on the tabletop.

"Just make sure that," Bruce pointed toward the piece of paper that Madison had left, "gets in tomorrow's paper. I don't want to be wearing cement galoshes anytime soon." He joked, but there was no smile on his face. The guy was serious and slightly pale as he hurried back to his office.

Jackie entered the info in the system and slumped in her chair. After a quick search of the web, several stories popped up about the Genoa Caponellis. Madison had owned a bridal store when she first met her husband. It was rumored that after Madison convinced a battered future bride to call off the wedding, the abusive fiancé soon disappeared. After that, several businesses in town had been vandalized, and there was even an explosion that destroyed part of the town. The suspect in those crimes was never found, just his hands.

Just his hands?

She sat up straight in her chair.

More crime stories had arisen since Roman had moved here. Whether that had anything to do with him, it was hard to tell. Genoa had a serial killer on the loose for a while. The psycho had struck in other states before shooting themselves in the head and leaving a suicide note behind in an abandoned building in town.

Wow.

Jackie bit her lip and continued to read. Then there were some meth deals gone bad. A lab that blew up outside of town, killing two inside. The apartment that author Stephanie Barclay lived in also blew up. How did Jackie not know these things? She'd done research before moving here but didn't remember coming across any of this. The last few years had been difficult, so it wasn't a surprise that she'd let things slip under the radar.

Jackie hit the search for images, and more popped up. Under the photo of Stephanie, the name Anastasia Bravikova appeared. It was believed that Bravikova was the daughter of a Russian mob boss from the West Coast who had relocated to Genoa. Jackie picked up a second pencil and tapped it on the desk. Her heart pounded. Writing classified ads and cat stories just wasn't cutting it, but stories like this were something she could sink her teeth into. This was what she was meant to write, but these stories had already been written.

Jackie brought up the page for Madison's winery again. The building, landscape, and vine fields were gorgeous. Like an Italian villa. It was the first time in a long time her inspiration flowed. The job description called for great customer service and attention to detail. Check and check. She had both of those. The applicant would be trained in all aspects of the wine industry. Check. She was trainable. She may have missed the boat on being a reporter, but this might be a new direction to take. Her days at the paper were probably numbered, so it didn't hurt to have other options on the table.

Next, she brought up the contact info for the job, filled it out, and attached her resume. Clicking the mouse, it was sent. If there was a story here, it would be found. She could publish it freelance, if need be. If not, she'd at least be enjoying a possible new career and much needed change of pace. Hopefully, the early bird would get the worm in this case. She'd apply before anyone else, and with any luck, Jackie'd be working at the winery soon.

Chapter Two

Jasper

The annoying as hell alarm on his phone wouldn't stop. After knocking several things off the table next to his bed, Jasper finally got ahold of it and stopped the noise. Why did he set it anyway? Rising in the morning had never been a problem before. For years, getting up and sneaking out of some hookup's bedroom from the night before was standard procedure. But that hadn't happened in a long time.

It'd been a dry spell for sure and a long, cold winter. He'd not been with a woman since last fall, to be exact. Everyone would be shocked, but it was true. Maybe it was seeing his now good friend, Dominic, find love. Something no one had expected. Jasper was happy for the couple, but sometimes, he felt like a third wheel whenever they got together.

Most people wouldn't guess what life had been like for him lately, as he'd hidden it well. He got up the same time every day, ate the same breakfast, watched the same news channel, and did the same workout routine. Well, most days, anyway. If he was working, that changed, but it didn't mean he had to like it.

Rubbing the back of his hand across his forehead, he yawned. Jasper rolled over and spread out in his bed. Alone. He was getting used to it, but that didn't mean he had to like it. For years, he'd been on the prowl; women, late nights, partying, nothing was off the table. He'd spent more time in other beds than his own. Never did he bring a guest to his place. That was too personal, too intimate. Plus, he liked the fact that he could leave when he wanted to. It wasn't that he was against commitment; it just wasn't for him. Commitment was for people who had emotions and who were sensitive, could feel things. That wasn't him. Killing came easy, and it always had.

In his line of work, it was best to be numb, and he'd been detached for a long time, without love and not giving a shit about the lack thereof. But somewhere over the winter, the urge to pursue and conquer had left the building. Hell, he didn't even know when it happened. Jasper just went home early from the bars or didn't even go out at all. Blame it on the weather; going out at night in twenty below weather was never fun. Maybe he was just maturing or growing up, as some would say. Hell, if Dom could find love, maybe he could too.

Dominic and Stephanie still invited him over, but sometimes, he'd say no. They were still in the honeymoon phase and so happy, unlike him. Jasper stared at the ceiling. He hadn't bothered to the hit the snooze button, but he didn't need it anyway. Tossing the covers aside, he dragged himself out of bed and into the bathroom.

After washing his face, he took a good, long look at the person staring back. Nothing appeared any different. He was still in great shape. All those workouts had carved out some pretty decent abs and the V that all the girls liked. Was he getting old? No, he was barely thirty.

What the hell?

Flipping off the light, he padded on bare feet to the kitchen. Jasper had even started programing the coffee maker to be ready in the morning. That was something he'd never done before. Why bother when he wasn't usually here in the morning? Pouring himself a cup, he searched the fridge for some flavored creamer and added some sugar. He may be on a dry spell, as far as the ladies were concerned, but he still had a sweet tooth.

Fixing oatmeal in the microwave and adding brown sugar, he took his breakfast to the living room and turned on the TV. The weatherman was predicting warmer days, and it was about time. They'd just had one of the coldest Aprils in history, and it was time to enjoy the lake.

Maybe seeing chicks in shorts and tank tops would get his blood flowing to all the right places again.

His cell rang, and he raced back to his room. It'd gone to voicemail, but he knew there'd be no message. The number was Roman's. People often didn't leave messages in his line of work. A text was sent. Just a set of numbers. 1015. It was an order to be at Roman's house at 10. Anything with a number and no letters was a request to be at his boss's house. Letters were abbreviations for places. Not obvious ones that enemies or the law would figure out, but ones that Roman's men would know by heart. If anyone figured out what they meant, they'd be fifteen minutes too late and not know what hit them. The clock on the wall said eight. He had a couple of hours to work out, shower, and be on his way.

No matter what was on the schedule for the day, Jasper liked to look good. Dressing to impress, or intimidate, often called for a nice suit. A pair of cufflinks, an ankle and shoulder holster, several knives, and a pair of brass knuckles completed his outfit. Grabbing his key fob and phone, he headed to the garage where his black Lexus SUV waited. Over the years, he'd been smart with his money and had a nice nest egg saved up. His only indulgences were the Lexus and his threads.

Jasper lived in a nice neighborhood only a few blocks from the lake. His rental was one of the many remodeled turn of the century homes in town. He had moved out of his downtown apartment last fall. This was much more to his liking of his new-found maturity, if one could call it that. There were security cameras around the home, and after a quick glance at the different views around his house from his phone, it looked like the coast was clear. Threats were minimal here in Genoa, but getting soft and complacent was never a good thing.

He drove the vehicle out of the garage and made

a quick detour at the Java Shop's drive-through. Sure, he'd already had a cup, but damn it was hard to wake up today. After setting the double mint espresso in the cup holder, he drove through the lot, only to see Valentina, Madison, and Oscar, their new bodyguard, getting into one of Roman's SUVs.

Jasper stopped and rolled down the window. "Hey."

The women both strolled over to say "hi."

"How's the little Caponelli doing?" He nodded to the baby in Valentina's car seat.

"Good try, Jasp. Don't let Ryan hear that. This baby's half Donavan."

"Someone has to keep the family growing." They all looked at Madison, except for the bodyguard, who was keeping his eye out for any threats.

"I know nothing of babies and clearly have no room in my life right now for one." Her face turned bright red, and she shook her head. "We're just starting the winery, not to mention everything else going on."

"Sure." Jasper nodded. He'd been of a part the mafia all his life, and there was no way Roman was not going to have an heir to carry on the legacy of his line. "Well, I have to get going. Ladies, have a great morning."

Driving to the exit of the parking lot, he hit the brakes harder than intended. There, coming out of the front door of the Java Shop, was a tall woman with long, red hair. His eyes widened, and without taking a sip of his coffee, Jasper was jolted awake. Even from a distance, it was hard to miss her slim figure and hot as hell legs. He'd always preferred blondes and brunettes, but she now held his interest like no one had in a long time. Even without seeing her face, there was something familiar about her.

A car behind him honked. Jasper cursed and let his foot off the brake. He turned right onto the street then circled around the block, hoping for another glimpse, but the girl was gone.

Dammit to hell.

Maybe there was something wrong with him, health-wise. Nobody'd been able to stir his blood in months, and just the mere glimpse of some strange woman in a parking lot had his heart beating like he'd just run a race. *Shit.* He was messed up for sure. Tonight, he was calling some friends, going out on the town, and getting laid. It was a done deal. End of story.

Shaking the cobwebs from his head, Jasper travelled the rest of the way through town and arrived at Roman's five minutes early. He recognized different cars in the lot. Arlo was there, as was Dominic.

At exactly ten o'clock, they all gathered in Roman's office. Everyone took a seat while their boss looked through a stack of papers in front of him. Roman set them aside and rested his elbows on the arms of his desk chair. The leather creaked as he settled back and crossed an ankle over his knee.

"I've a few jobs for you to do today. As you know since we've been here, collections have been up, and we've not had any problems with payments." Roman placed his foot on the floor and leaned forward. "Until now." He handed each man a sheet of paper.

"This guy is in over his head by half a mil. I need Jasper and Arlo to make a visit today. The address is on there."

Jasper glanced at the picture on the sheet, and his jaw nearly dropped. "Isn't this—"

"It is," Roman interrupted. "The guy's been living beyond his means for a long time. I want his accounts up to date no later than tomorrow."

Jasper studied the photo again. It was Rodney Studd. The man was the lead guitarist of a rock band that'd been around for years. They weren't, and hadn't been for a while, major players on the music scene, but apparently, no one had told his wallet. Being in debt to the mob for five zeros meant Studd's life was going to get a lot more interesting.

"What's his reason for being late?" Jasper may not have a heart, but he was never a fan of going after people with health issues or family problems.

"Like I said, he's been living beyond his means. High-priced women, high-end art, gambling, you name it. Old habits die hard, and they haven't had a hit in a long time."

"What if he won't pay?" Arlo asked.

"You know what to do." Roman sighed and began flipping through another pile of papers. It was going to be a busy day, if that was any indication.

"Yes, but if we break his hands or remove the fingers from a guitar player, he'll never pay up." Arlo was always the practical one.

"I trust you'll be able to figure it out." Roman

passed out a few more papers with addresses and photos of those who needed to be contacted about overdue debts. They wouldn't be leaving the room with these sheets, so it was important to memorize the names, faces, and addresses.

There was a local mechanic with a gambling problem, a district attorney who lost big in the stock market, and a deadbeat father of six with an expensive girlfriend on the side.

"You planning on offing any of these?" Dominic took his stack over to the shredder and started to feed them through.

"No." Roman looked at his watch. "Not yet anyway. I prefer to work things out and get repeat business."

"Then why am I here?" Dom was never one to mince works.

"I want you at the winery as much as possible."

"Winery?" His friend returned to the chair by Jasper's side.

"Yeah. As you've probably heard, Madison wants to take this family legit as much as possible. I'm all for that, but we still have to make money, a lot of money. And that doesn't happen overnight. That place cost me a fucking fortune, and until it starts to make a profit, the legal alcohol will go out the front door and the bootleg stuff will be going out the back."

"Wait a minute. Bootleg?" Jasper chuckled. "This isn't prohibition."

"No, but there are still a lot of regulations for the sales of alcohol. There are some that can only be sold in certain states, and we have buyers in others.

It also won't be just wine going through those doors."

The guys were silent, and Roman explained further. "Madison is not to know. She's not to get involved in any of this. I love my wife and want to protect her, but like I said, we're in the business to make money, and if we want to stay here, we have to keep our profits up."

It was well-known that Roman's father wasn't happy about his two children leaving Chicago and Roman setting up turf elsewhere.

"Dominic, I want you to be the handyman around the place. Keep an eye on things. Make some fucking iron wine holders, for all I care." Roman laughed, but everyone knew Dominic, in addition to being the mob's cleaner, was a talented artist when it came to metal work. "Your job is to keep watch over the workers. There's a hidden room with a tunnel to the outside. Jasper," his boss turned his attention toward him, "you, Arlo, and I will have the only keys. The tunnel goes a half mile, and the other entrance is on someone else's property. That's where the trucks will load and unload the hooch and any other items we'll be transporting."

Jasper smirked. "Hooch?" It was a term used to describe illegal alcohol during prohibition. "I'm going to invest in a fedora and a tommy gun. Ladies love a gangster."

"Not unless you're going to the speakeasy in town. We need to keep this quiet. I don't plan on going to jail or divorce court."

Everyone nodded. They had it good here and

didn't want to lose what they had.

"You said that the tunnel ended on someone else's property." This time it was Arlo who spoke up. "Who's property?"

"District Attorney Velasco. He's on your list and can't pay. It shouldn't be a problem to use the right of way on his land." Roman smiled. "Dom, you're with me today. Arlo and Jasp, get these collections made. I don't care if you have to cut off Studd's arm. I want to be paid."

Chapter Three

Jasper

Rodney Studd's place was typical for the homes around the lake. Lots of square footage and expensive. Actually, it was probably one of the largest estates there.

Arlo whistled as he got out of the car. "The bigger they are, the harder they fall."

"Ain't that the truth." Jasper slammed the door and buttoned his suitcoat. They'd been let in down by the gate, so Studd obviously knew they were coming. The man had been told his debt was due, and now it was time to deliver that message in person. Sometimes doing that in the bright light of day was just as intimidating as shaking someone down in a dark parking lot. Image meant everything to celebs. No one wanted two made men from the mob showing up for all the paparazzi to see.

The front door opened before they even walked up the stairs. It was Rodney. Overly tanned, overly bleached blonde, and he was dressed in only a small speedo. The years had not been kind to the rocker. The lines in his face were numerous and deep, like a roadmap of one's travels and hardships throughout life. The man had obviously indulged in various types of illegal drugs throughout the years. His hands shook, and he almost seemed to be panting.

Anxious much?

"Gentlemen, come in, come in." Rod dramatically and hurriedly waved them in, which triggered Arlo and Jasp to take even slower steps.

"I'm Rod. What can I do for you?" He shut the door as soon as they were inside. The interior of his house opened to a huge room that basically held nothing. It was just a wide-open space with doors going to other parts of the house and two open stairways.

Arlo spoke first. "Cut the bullshit. You know who we are and that we're here on behalf of Mr. Caponelli."

"Ah, yes, yes. Please," again with the waving of the arms, "follow me to my office." Rod took off down a hallway, and they trailed behind.

The foyer behind them may have been empty, but every space on the walls in the hallway was filled with paintings. Jasper stopped at one. He was no art connoisseur, but a few he was pretty sure he'd seen on TV or in a book somewhere. As soon as they were in the office, Studd ushered them to sit. Arlo walked toward the desk, but Jasper continued to study the art pieces on the wall. These were all familiar, and the signature on one said Picasso.

"Your payment is due, Studd." Arlo settled into a chair and rested his ankle over one knee. "We're here to collect."

"Well, now." Rodney scratched his head. He must have known they were coming, yet now he seemed to be in shock at the news. "Is it that time already?"

"Did you think this was a social call? Do you always invite guys in off the street to your home?" Arlo cracked his knuckles. "Are you going to pay up, or do we need to break something?"

"Now, now. Gentlemen." Rodney paled, and his eyes darted around the room. "You see, things have been a little tight the last few years. Sales are down. Too many ex-wives, child support." He shook his head, walked over to the bar, and poured himself a drink. Didn't everyone have a bar in their office? Rodney Studd did, and he drained the dark liquid in the glass in one gulp. "I can't pay. Everything's tied up in my latest divorce. They froze everything. I even had to let most of the staff go." His face seemed to add another wrinkle with that statement. "I mow the lawn in the middle of the night so no one can see it's me doing it."

"I'm crying inside." Arlo stood up. "We aren't leaving empty handed. Pay up or face the consequences."

"Please, I got a tour coming up. When that's done, I can give you the money from that. Even pay extra." His eyes widened.

"Sorry, but the boss wants payment today." Arlo pressed a fist into his palm.

"I've got nothing," Studd pleaded, his hands folded in prayer, then he pointed toward his laptop. "Take a look. My bank account's empty. I'm tapped out. That's why I borrowed in the first place."

"Well, I hope you still have health insurance, as I see a visit to the doctor in your future." Arlo started around the desk. "Maybe you can collect on the insurance for your accident."

"What accident?" Rodney's brown face turned as white as his hair, and he backed up against the wall.

"The one you're about to have."

Arlo was scary on a good day. The guy was huge, and everyone often joked that he should be a blocker for the Packers. To see him coming their direction would make any man pee in his shorts, but making a man unable to work wouldn't get his payments down.

"Wait," Jasper called, and both men turned his way. "I think I have an idea."

Jackie

It'd been three weeks since Mrs. Caponelli had walked into the Genoa Globe to drop off her help wanted ad. Two days after emailing her resume, Jackie had been asked to meet for an interview. Surprising it hadn't been at the winery but at the coffee shop where she'd first laid eyes on the person that would hopefully be her new boss.

The conversation had gone well, but then one never knew about these things. There may have been more qualified candidates seen before or after her. It was hard to contain the happy dance at work when Madison called her the following Monday to let her know the job was hers. After hearing the good news, she'd marched into the news station and had given her notice. Bruce was not happy, to say the least, and even tried to talk her out of it.

Today, she would finally start a new beginning. Not sure what she'd be doing on her first day, Jackie dressed conservatively in a pair of dress khakis and a crisp periwinkle shirt. The day was bright and sunny, which matched perfectly how she felt. It was great to get out of town, even if the winery was only a couple miles outside of the city limits, and enjoy the countryside. Starting a new job was always nerve-wracking, but it was equally exciting. Her stomach had been in knots all morning. Wanting to look perfect, she'd barely had time to get a coffee and bagel down and throw a few energy bars in her bag for lunch.

Jackie had hoped to do a little more research on the place, but after first checking out the website at work, it had been off-line ever since. Probably because of the new ownership. The place had looked beautiful on screen, but would it be the same in person? She wondered this before turning the corner and traveling over to the hill.

It was and more. Breathtaking would be an understatement. La Bella Luna winery was stunning. It was easy to imagine one's self in Italy as she traveled down the tree-lined driveway. The tasting room and main building were Mediterranean in style. They featured red tile roofs and stone exterior. Jackie parked in the lot, grabbed her purse, and headed in the front door. The inside was just as nice, with light walls and dark wood accents.

"Good morning." Madison sat at a table with a handsome older gentleman, who stood as she neared. "Alain, this is Jackie. She'll be my right hand soon and will be taking over some of the PR duties, as well as helping me oversee operations."

Jackie wasn't quite sure what her new job entailed yet, but her resume listed her as experienced in anything and everything. Hopefully, she hadn't stretched things beyond her capabilities. She always considered herself a fast learner, so she'd be putting that to the test in the coming days.

Alain held out a chair, and Jackie took a seat. There was already a pad, paper, and new laptop in front of her.

"This is yours for work. I'll show you to your office as soon as we're done. First, we will go over your responsibilities. I'm new to this venture as well, but Alain worked here with the previous owners for years and knows everything about growing grapes and producing high quality wines. He's stayed on and will be helping with the transition."

For the next few hours, Jackie took notes as they toured the place. Alain had given them a brief description of the working parts of the winery and showed them all the different types of grapes they harvested. They grew three kinds there, one for red wine, one for white wine, and one for rosé. Being in the Midwest, the grapes had a faster growing season than those in warmer climates. Her new office was next to Madison's, and it had a wonderful view of the surrounding hills. They then returned to the tasting room, where Alain excused himself to get back to work.

Since Jackie worked at the newspaper, Madison

wanted her to come up with local, state, and regional contacts for a press release. Her boss used to work with the local tourism department, so they had a great list to start with already. The wine they served and sold was from previous harvests. There was room for a small restaurant that was once used to serve pizza. It was also big enough to host intimate gatherings, but Madison explained that they wouldn't be doing that. For now, they had to get things changed over to the new name and brand.

Eventually, there would be wine tastings, and they'd also be selling cheeses and other local products for sale. The family owned a big restaurant called Firenza, so there was no use having another restaurant and place to hold events. They had enough on their plate. This would strictly be a wine-producing site for now.

The former restaurant would soon be sized down for a break and meeting room for employees.

"Because of the construction, we won't be able to hold wine tastings here for a month or so." Madison glanced at her phone.

"If we aren't serving it here, how will people get to try it?" It could be done, but it didn't seem like that best of ideas.

"It will be sold at Firenza and other places in town, such as grocery and liquor stores, which are already carrying it." Madison smiled. It didn't take Jackie long to realize that her boss really did know what she was doing. Jackie's boss had dressed similar to her, only she was dressed in black pants and a white shirt. The colors would be horrible on Jackie, but they complimented the woman's dark hair and porcelain skin to perfection. She also wore simple pearl stud earrings, and the diamond ring on her finger had to weigh a ton.

"What about hosting a charity event to promote the winery?" Jackie marked a number one in ink on her paper.

"I knew we'd get along well. I've got a small one lined up in a few days to be our grand opening, so to speak."

"What? Really?" She began tapping her pen on the table. This day kept getting better and better.

"Yes, it will be at Firenza. Kind of a ladies' night. Wine, cheese, chocolate, and some kind of raffle or auction to raise money." Madison listed a short menu they could use and the types of wines they had to pair with them.

"We would have a tasting first to get people loosened up. A flight of five of the wines that we will spotlight should do just fine. After that, they can buy more, if they want. In keeping with the fun theme for the evening, the charity would be for the local humane society or something. Everyone loves puppies and kittens."

"Now, what kind of an auction are you thinking?" Jackie twirled her pen in her fingers. It was exciting to be in on the ground floor of starting something new and fresh.

"We could've asked for donations, but I had another idea in mind." There was a mischievous look on Madison's face.

"What?" This event sounded more fun by the minute. "From the expression on your face, it sounds intriguing."

"Tell me, Jackie. Do you have a boyfriend?" Madison crossed her arms in front of her chest.

That was the last thing Jackie expected to hear.

"Huh? Boyfriend?" She shook her head. "No, I haven't been in town long enough to meet anyone, and with work and all…" Actually, she'd been here since late summer but preferred to find her boyfriends between the pages of a book. "Ah, why?"

"I thought about having a bachelor auction." Madison beamed.

"Bachelors? Like win a date with so and so?"

Bachelor auctions? Hadn't that gone out in the eighties?

"Yes. You bid on the person you wish to take to dinner at Firenza. The meal is included. I think it will be fun. They'd have to be single, of course."

"Of course." Jackie wasn't buying it. With the current state of political correctness, who would want to do such a thing? It was genius, though. Women loved wine, animals, and food. They would also get to pick a handsome man to enjoy it with.

"I know everyone meets on the internet today, but when you live in a small town, the person you're looking for could be right next door and you don't even know it." Madison placed her elbows on the table and interlocked her fingers. "This is a tourist town. Half the year, it's filled with people who aren't from here, which makes it even harder to find someone that you're meant to be with."

"Yeah, that makes sense, but where are we going to get the bachelors?" Jackie was warming up to the idea.

"You let me worry about that." The front door opened and closed. "Here's one right now."

She thought it was Alain coming back in, but it was a young man. Well, a man that appeared to be around her age or a few years older. Jackie started at his shiny shoes and gave him the once over. He was a sharp dresser, that's for sure. The navy suit looked custom made and expensive; so were the sunglasses the man pushed up until they settled in the thick of his black hair. The man was tall and slender, but the suit showed off the muscular frame of his body to perfection. However, it was his deep brown eyes that held her captive. They seemed to see right through her. The man had a face that would make women of all ages stop for a second look. A straight nose, full lips, and strong jaw. The whole package screamed mischief and mystery, while the scruffy five o'clock shadow raised the sexiness level to the top of the scale.

"Here's one what?" Even the guy's voice was tasty and rich, just like chocolate milk. Jackie unconsciously licked her lips. Was it hot in here?

"I need you to volunteer to be one of the bachelors in my auction for charity," Madison told him.

"What?" The guy pulled out a chair and straddled it. "Maddy, no way." His light aftershave invaded her space, but instead of causing her allergies to kick in, it caused her to lean closer. There was something familiar about him, but she couldn't place it.

"Please," Madison begged. "It's for a good cause."

"What cause?" He scratched his chin, and the raspy sound of it tickled spots on her skin that had no business being entertained on the first day of a job.

"It's for the Humane Society. You like cats and dogs."

"You know I love pussy." The man had the nerve to wink at Jackie. It should have been a warning that that man was a tease, but she actually had to place her hand in front of her mouth to hide the gasp that formed on her lips. He was a player, that was for sure.

"Jasper!" Madison tossed a pencil at him. "Just for that, you have to do this. Get me some names of other guys also. I'm thinking Arlo would be good. I'll get Layla to bid on him." She listed a few more names, but the man in front of them just exhaled and shook his head. "Wait, where are my manners? Jackie, this is Jasper. Jasper, this is Jacqueline Smith."

He stood and reached over to shake her hand. "Nice to meet you. Jaclyn Smith was always my favorite angel. You know, on *Charlie's Angels*."

Jackie also rose and took his hand. It was warm and strong and made her cozy all over. "Right. Same name, different spelling." Then it hit her: they had met before. "Pleasure to meet you."

"Pleasure's all mine." Jasper didn't let go. "Wait. Do I know you?"

Chapter Four

Jasper

It came back in a flash. He knew this woman. Well, not as much as he'd liked to, but they'd met last fall at Stephanie's book signing. She was a reporter. He dropped her hand. Journalists were the worst, so why was she here talking to Maddy?

"Don't you work for the paper?" The last thing they needed was someone nosing around the place.

"I used to. Then, one morning, Madison came in to place her help-wanted ad for the winery, and I was lucky enough to get the job. It was time for a change." She tilted her head to the side, and a thick strand of red hair fell across one eye until she brushed it away with graceful fingers. What the hell? Graceful fingers? He'd had too much coffee if he was noticing people's digits. She was a hottie, though, and hard to forget. Her rejection last fall when he'd asked her out on a date still burned.

Out of nowhere, it dawned on him that that was when his downward spiral had started, and she was probably to blame. It both bugged and intrigued him. Until now, he'd not even given her a second thought.

"You were the first to apply." Her boss spoke up. "I wasn't sure I'd get any capable people, so I was excited about Jackie's experience in writing, advertising, and organization skills."

"So, you're no longer a reporter?"

It'd be great if she wasn't.

"Nope. The only stories I wrote at the paper were fluff, anyway. Nothing exciting ever seems to happen around here." Jackie picked up her pen and twirled it around her fingers.

His gaze locked on Maddy's for a moment. If her new hire only knew all the stuff that took place in their territory. "Where are you from?" Jasper took a seat again.

"Chicago, but I went to school at the University of Madison for journalism. The job wasn't what I thought it would be." Her gaze lowered to the table.

"Good." Jasper stopped. "I mean, it's not good that it didn't work out but that you're moving on to bigger and better things. Hopefully. That is. Now here. At the winery." He couldn't recall ever stuttering before. So uncool.

"Jasp, what are you rattling on about?" Madison teased.

"You know how your husband feels about the press. He wouldn't be happy about a reporter working here." That would be the last thing they needed. "No one likes gossip."

"I'm sorry. What?" Jackie frowned.

"It's nothing." Madison shook her head. "My

husband is kind of high-profile and hates attention. Let me worry about him." The front door opened, and they all turned. It was his boss, followed by Arlo and Dominic.

"Looks like the whole crew is here now." Madison stood, and Roman kissed her cheek. "Jackie, I'd like you meet my husband, Roman. And this is Arlo and Dominic."

Jackie stood, greeted, and shook hands with each but only spoke to Dom. "I was there at your wife's book signing last fall. You'd just proposed. It was one of the most romantic things I'd ever seen. Do you have a brother?" she joked.

Dominic just shrugged it off. "We aren't married yet. Soon."

"Well, you made her very happy. Anyone could see that." Jackie blushed.

Jasper remembered that moment. Everyone had stood in line for Stephanie to sign their book, but when Dom showed up, he'd handed her one that was already inscribed. Dominic's heartfelt message to Stephanie was written inside. It was then that he got down on one knee and proposed. All the ladies in the room swooned, and all the men thought, how the hell do you top that?

He studied the young woman giving Dom the attention and did a double take. It wasn't just last fall that he'd seen her; it was a couple weeks ago. He'd bet his left nut that she was the beauty walking down the sidewalk. There weren't many redheads in town, and this chick was the right height and had the same length hair.

"Do you ever go to the Java Shop?" he blurted

out, and everyone glanced at him like he'd grown another head.

"Me?" Jackie placed her left hand on her chest, and he almost jumped with joy that there was no ring there. Damn, there he was gawking at fingers again. "Ah, yes. Why?"

"No reason. I just saw someone leaving there a couple weeks ago and just now thought it might have been you."

"I used to stop by there on the way to work. I just live a few blocks away." Jackie took her seat again. "What? Did I fall on my face or something for you to remember me?"

"No. I just remembered the hair. You know what they say, don't ya?"

She just shook her head and stared.

"Gentlemen prefer blondes, but real men prefer redheads." Jackie blushed and looked everywhere but at him. As soon as he got home, he'd have the tech guys get him her address.

Stalker much?

The others rolled their eyes or groaned until Roman finally said something.

"It was nice meeting you, Jackie. I hope you'll feel at home here and enjoy your time working with my wife."

"Thank you. I'm sure I will." Her cheeks pinked even more with all the attention switched to her.

"So, why are you all here?" Madison sat back down next to Jackie.

"I'm having the guys check out the storage rooms. I know everything's been inspected, but I'm just double checking to see if anything else needs to be done so it's all up to code. Dom's going to work on that railing that's loose and go over the plans for the break room."

"All right. Thanks for doing that, guys. We won't keep you." They started to leave, but she stopped them. "Oh, and Arlo, I have something to ask. It's about the charity event. I need you there next week and any of the other guys you can spare." She smiled at her husband.

Roman put his hands in his pockets. "When is this?"

"Next week. I need some bachelors for a charity auction."

"Oh, hell no," Arlo spoke up.

"Come on. I'll make sure Layla bids on you." She winked.

Arlo was huge. Nothing seemed to rile him, but this had him tugging at the collar of his shirt.

"Sorry. I need him that night," Roman said, and Arlo sighed.

"But—" Madison started.

"No buts. We're busy." Roman's word was final.

"Where am I going to find enough guys in that short amount of time?" Madison was clearly panicked, but Roman just shrugged.

"We could contact the local police and fire department for any single men that might be interested in helping," Jackie volunteered.

"There you go. Sounds like Jackie has it all taken care of." Roman turned to leave.

"But—" Madison said again.

"No buts. You can have Jasper, but that's it," her husband replied firmly.

"What? I never said I'd do it," Jasper sputtered. He loved attention, but having a bunch of rich society ladies bid for a date with him was just messed up. It seemed almost desperate.

"You'll do it." His boss pointed his way.

Jasper exhaled and hung his head. You didn't argue with Roman. Ever.

"Now, let's go. We've work to do." Roman led the way. Everyone knew that what Madison wanted, Madison usually got. She rarely did ask, but it was a sign of respect to their boss. If she asked Jasper to dance naked on the table, he'd be stripping now. Fortunately, it was only a charity auction. With his luck, it'd be some rich older women that won a date with him. Not that he didn't appreciate a woman of experience, but as he took a quick glance back before he exited the room, he kind of had a hot redhead in mind.

Jasper pointed at Madison. "We'll talk later." She just smiled and waved.

The winery had some big tanks and vats. He knew shit about wine making, but it seemed pretty scientific. Everything was either stainless steel or wooden. No one spoke as they passed all the equipment and into a storage room. That space had arches on all the walls that looked like openings to other areas, but they were fake. All except for the one in which Roman removed an ornamental piece of trim and inserted a key. A door shifted out, and they walked into a hidden room.

Once it was closed behind them, Roman addressed the men.

"Dom, I've added you to the list of keyholders,

since you might be here more than the others. Most of the stuff will be coming in from the other way and stored here, but sometimes, we will need to get things from this side as well."

There were various crates and other items covered by drop cloths about the room.

"That brings me to this." Jasper swallowed as Roman pulled up a painting and set it on the table. "That was quick thinking on the Studd deal."

Roman removed the covering to reveal one of the rocker's prized paintings. "He gets to collect the insurance money for it being stolen. We will be getting part of the cash. We also get to sell this piece, which should go for well over a million."

"How will we sell something that's this famous and listed as stolen?" Dominic scratched his head. "It's a fucking Picasso."

"The tech guys have a site on the dark web. A type of lost and found, so to speak. Studd lost it, and we found it, so we're selling it. We also have the option for people to request things that we might be able to find as well." Roman rested his backside on a nearby desk.

"Won't the police be investigating the theft?" Arlo folded his arms in front of him.

"Yes, they will be, and they will find nothing of suspect on any of the security tapes. The tech guys have taken care of sweeping them clean during any of our visits." Roman had thought of everything.

"So, we're art dealers now?" Jasper knew the painting was valuable, but it wasn't his taste, that was for sure.

"That and other things. Guns, jewels, gold. There

are certain wine, beer, and alcohol that's only available for sale in this state also. We're going to bypass that here. Anything our clients want, within reason, we'll get it for them." Roman smiled. "At a very high price, that is."

"Art dealers and bootleggers." Jasper laughed. "Never a dull moment."

"What if they want something we can't get? It's not like everyone that owes us money is going to have expensive art to just hand over?" Dominic leaned against the wall. He was dressed in his usual jeans, t-shirt, and flannel shirt. Or, as Stephanie called it, the "cross between a serial killer and hot lumberjack" look.

For the next couple hours, Roman went over more of the details for the operation. They had several details to work out, but they would also be getting a new member of the family soon—a highly paid, highly sought-after jewel thief.

"When's this person coming?"

"Soon. They're in Europe right now. Acquiring a few orders that have been placed already."

Jasper met Dom's gaze. Things were changing all the time. Technology was making old ways out of date, and they had to adapt to keep up.

"Any questions?" Their boss stood and made eye contact with each man.

"No, but if anything comes up, I'll be sure to ask." Jasper shoved a hand into his pants pocket. The other two men just shook their heads.

"Okay, let's go. Dom and Arlo, you come with me, and I'll show you the other entrance. Jasp, you stay here with Maddy."

They followed him out, and the three left, leaving only Jasper and Madison still out front.

"Where's the new girl?" He took the chair that Jackie had been sitting in. Her subtle perfume still lingered. It was citrusy mixed with the scent of flowers.

"Since I need guys, I sent her with a flyer to the cop shop and fire station." She rested her jaw on her fist. "At least I have you signed up."

"About that." Jasper smiled.

"Yeah?" She lifted one eyebrow.

"I'll do it on one condition."

Madison exhaled. "And what's that?"

"You have to make sure Jackie Smith bids on me and wins."

Chapter Five

Jasper

It was another collection day. They only had five stops, and they didn't include any celebrities or aging rock stars. Ordinary people were much easier. No cameras or security guards to catch them visiting the premises. The tech guy always let them know first if there was any surveillance in the areas anyway.

Arlo rode shotgun today. The big guy was in one of his moods. Jasper preferred working with Dominic, but with someone always needing to be with Maddy at the winery, they didn't have much of a choice. There were other soldiers on the payroll, but Roman only trusted a few with his precious wife, and Oscar must have been needed elsewhere today. Dom would be with her all morning while they made their stops.

Lucky bastard.

Jasper wouldn't mind more shifts there, as he could hopefully get closer to Jackie.

Collections were easy. Take payment or dole out punishment. However, if they didn't have the money, it was sometimes a bitch finding the person. The family lent money at high interest. These days, most people in a pinch could go to the bank or just put things on a credit card, but if they were into things that required cash only or didn't have that option, the Caponellis were their new best friend. If they could pay them back, that was. If they couldn't, then they were their worst enemy.

The first time the debtor didn't cough up the money, it was a warning. Maybe just verbal, sometimes a physical reminder if they became belligerent. The second time always left a mark and often involved a body part being removed or broken. Often a finger or, if the person needed all digits to make money, a toe nipped or a knee bent might be the better option. One guy offered up his ear. That was messy and ruined a nice jacket Jasper loved.

This was old school mob shit, but it was effective. People were too soft these days. Everyone still thought they could just plead their case and get off easy. The mob never let anyone off easy. That showed weakness and was bad for business. There was no begging or filing for chapter thirteen if they didn't have the funds.

One of their stops today would be the person's third visit. If they didn't pay, he'd be dead. That's why Dom worked at Madison's place in the morning. If needed, he'd be free to clean up their messes later in the day.

"Who's first?" Jasper rubbed his jaw.

"Ricky," Arlo grumbled.

"I hate that dick." Jasper had a knack for identifying lowlifes, and this guy made a snake appear tall.

"Agreed." Richard Harrison was a jerk. Hopefully, he wouldn't pay, and they could rid the world of the bastard. "I called the garage he works at, but they said he was home sick today."

"Guess we'll be making a house call, then." Jasper scratched his chin and stepped on the gas.

They drove out of town and down a long winding road. Ricky lived with his wife in an old farmhouse. By the look of it, it'd seen its better days back in the twenties or earlier.

They parked, and Jasper walked to the front door, while Arlo went around back. If they had a runner, they wouldn't get far.

Standing to the side of the door, Jasper knocked and waited. It wouldn't be the first time someone shot through a door. He wasn't taking any chances.

"I'm coming," someone hollered, and their footsteps could be heard creaking on the weak floor from inside. A blonde woman answered, but he couldn't see her face.

"Richard home today?" Jasper tried to see inside.

"Who wants to know?" She still wouldn't meet his eyes.

"He owes me some money, and I'm here to collect." The woman frowned and finally raised her gaze to meet his. A bruise had recently formed on her face. It was a nasty red color, and her swollen eye watered. There were also a few cuts on her cheekbones. The kind fighters get when a fist

51

causes the skin to split. Jasper tightened his fists. If Ricky did this, his death would be painful and drawn out, for sure. "Did he do this?" He spoke so only she could hear, but the door was suddenly flung open before she could answer.

"Hey, I was just on my way to see you. Thanks for saving me a trip." It was Richard. His cheeks were red, and the pupils of his eyes twitched. Only ten in the morning and he was already drunk as a skunk.

The man slapped a wad of wet cash in Jasper's hand. He was sweaty and smelled of booze and cigarettes. Flipping through the bills, Jasper was never so disappointed to have someone pay in full. Even the interest was accounted for.

Damn.

"It's all there." The man belched and crushed a beer can in his hand. "Anything else?" Yeah, Jasper wanted to crush the guy's skull.

"No. We're square." The door slammed shut. Jasper folded the cash and stuffed it into his pocket. It was time to leave, but he couldn't get his feet to move.

"Let's go." Arlo was back by the car, and Jasper finally headed his way.

"You drive." Jasper threw him the keys and climbed into the passenger seat this time. "Did you see anyone else in there?"

"No, just the two." He started the car, and they traveled back down the road, keeping an eye on the rearview mirror. Neither would put it past the guy to shoot them in the back.

"That his wife?" Jasper crossed his arms over his

chest. The urge to give Ricky a black eye burned in his chest.

"As far as I know. I knew Rick was a no-good prick, but I never heard any word about him being abusive," Arlo grumbled. He must have glimpsed her from the window as well.

"Money problems cause people to do stupid things, but that's never an excuse to hit a woman." Jasper shook his head.

"Agreed. I was hoping he wouldn't pay."

"Me too, but it's all here." He patted his pocket.

"We could throw it out the window," Arlo joked.

"Yeah." Jasper chuckled. "Wonder where it came from? He didn't have it the last two times, and suddenly, it's all accounted for."

"Hard to tell." Arlo raised his hands off the wheel as he shrugged his shoulders.

The rest of the morning went just as easy. Each person paid, and it looked like Dominic would be having the afternoon off.

It was almost one o'clock when Jasper strolled into the winery. Ricky's wife still weighed heavy on his mind, but there was nothing he could do. Maybe she really had fallen and he was mistaken that the injuries had been caused by Rick, but it was doubtful.

"Hey, Angel." Jasper wandered into Jackie's office and set a cup and bag from the Java Shop on her desk. "I stopped in for coffee and thought you'd like one too."

"Wow." Her eyes widened, and she dropped the pen on the desk. "Ah. Thank you. That was really nice of you." She peeked in the bag. "My favorite.

You should play the lottery. You guessed spot on."

"No, I didn't." He lowered himself into the chair in front of her desk. "I asked if they knew you. They told me which drink and pastry you liked the best." Jasper shrugged. "The many joys of living in a small town. Everyone knows your business."

"Yes." She took a sip of the cappuccino. "Caramel mocha with vanilla. Thanks again, but you really didn't need to do that." Her smile made it all worthwhile.

"Yeah, well, I had an ulterior motive."

"Really?" Her pretty eyes looked up over the top of the mug.

"I was wondering if you might be free tomorrow night." He flashed her a grin.

"Why?" She focused on her laptop again before glancing back his way. Her brown eyes were a soft hazel, and there were a few freckles on her nose and cheeks.

"I'd like to take you to dinner." He smiled, lowered his chin, and glanced up. That move always seemed to work on the ladies, for some reason. The kind of puppy dog look they loved. Her cheeks pinkened, and the freckles drew his eyes. Talk about puppy dog. He was the lovesick one. First, he noticed her fingers. Now, he was checking out her freckles.

Jackie coughed and dabbed her lips with a napkin. She had the prettiest lips, and they'd look great working their way across his body. And that thick dark red hair. It looked so shiny and smooth. His hands itched to reach out and touch the silky strands.

"I can't." Her voice interrupted his daydream.

"Other plans?" Jasper flicked at a piece of lint that had worked under his fingernail. "Are you seeing anyone?"

"No and no." She took a bite of the pastry.

Jasper almost groaned when she licked the powdered sugar from her mouth. "So, why not go out?"

"Because I've heard you're a major player." Jackie narrowed her eyes. "I don't do one-night stands."

He placed a hand on his heart and raised his eyebrows. "Me? Where did you hear something like that?"

"From everyone. Like you just said, 'the many joys of living in a small town.' Your reputation is well known. Is there anyone in this county you haven't gone out with?" Her eyes were wide and her cheeks an even brighter pink.

"Yeah, you." Jasper leaned forward and rested his elbows on his knees.

"Well, I'm sorry, but like I said, I have no interest in casual hookups."

"And you think that's all I'm looking for?"

She lifted one eyebrow. "Isn't it?"

"No. I've matured." He winked, and she rolled her eyes. "Everyone has a past, but I see you in my future."

Her mouth opened, but she paused before speaking. "You're quite the charmer, Jasper, but I'm looking for a man who will treat me like my father did my mother. She was his world. They loved each other more than anything. I won't settle for anything else."

"Me too."

"Oh, please." She laughed but not in a condescending way.

"No. Hear me out. Isn't everyone looking for a love like that? Come on. Just give me a chance." He straightened back in his seat. "Maybe I'm the man for you."

"I doubt it." Jackie smiled and picked up her phone. "But thanks again for the snack."

"It's okay." He was being dismissed, and Jasper rose to his feet. "So, there's really no way you will go out with me?"

"Nope. Not ever." She said it, but did she really mean it?

"Ouch. That hurt." He leaned against the doorway.

"Sorry, but you're just not my type."

And what was her type? Jackie still hadn't looked up from her phone.

"I'll make you a bet." He wasn't giving up.

"What? A bet?" That seemed to get her attention, and she met his gaze. "Why?"

"Because I don't give up, and I think we'd be good together." Jackie still didn't look convinced. "I bet in one week you'll go on a date with me." He would need Madison's help with that one.

"No, I won't." She smiled.

"No, you won't go out, or no, you won't take the bet?"

"Both." Jackie leaned back in her chair and crossed one leg over the other.

"Well, I guess you're not the woman I thought

you were. I thought you were more adventurous." He wiggled his eyebrows. "Makes me think you don't want to take the bet because you know you'll cave."

"What? Never." Jackie put her cell down and crossed her arms in front of her chest. She was wearing a sleeveless green sweater that made her light skin appear golden.

"Then it's a bet." He held out his hand to seal the deal. "If you agree to go on a date with me, you have to go on a second one."

She wrinkled up her nose. "Ah, sure. I'm not going to, so what do I win?"

"Free coffee and pastry from the Java Shop every day for a month."

"This is crazy." Jackie laughed. "I'll get fat if I eat there every day."

"Okay, any day you want for two months." He smiled. The woman didn't know who she was up against. "Deal?"

She finally got to her feet and took his hand. "Deal."

Jasper bent at the waist and kissed the top of her hand. "I like a deal that's sealed with a kiss. Next time, it'll be on the lips."

The look on her face was priceless. It was a mixture of surprise and attraction, but he knew she'd never admit it. Her skin was flushed. She pulled her hand back and stuck it in her pocket.

"I look forward to our date. Both of them." He turned to leave but then stopped. "See you later, Angel."

***

Jackie

"If I'm an angel, then he's the devil." A demon with a breathtaking smile and tons of charisma. Jasper had caught her eye last year at the book signing. A coworker noticed her staring and was quick to share his reputation with the ladies. Jackie couldn't blame the women that lined up to date him. Date? From what she'd heard, it was usually only one night, yet there was never a bad comment said about the man. There were no scorned ex-girlfriends, that she'd heard about anyway. That didn't excuse the fact that the guy was obviously involved in illegal activities if he worked for the Caponellis.

Heck, she worked for a mob boss's wife. Something Jackie said she never would do. Ever. The woman had bodyguards, for goodness sake. And yet, here she was, an employee of one of their businesses, and loving every minute of her new job.

"Jackie?" Madison just buzzed her.

"Yes?"

"Can you find Jasper? I need him to help me with something, but I'm waiting for a call. I just saw him head toward the storage room."

"Sure, I'll go there right now." Jackie took one more drink from her coffee cup. It was a thoughtful thing for him to do, but she still wasn't going to let it persuade her.

Jackie wore heels today, as she knew they would be working inside. Her heels clicked on the tile as she went in search of Jasper. The lights were on in the large room, but he was nowhere in sight. "Huh." She called out his name, but the place was empty.

Madison must have been mistaken because this was the only way out and he was nowhere in sight.

Chapter Six

Jasper

The next day, he was back at the winery. Their secret store room had filled up nicely. Jewelry, furs, and guns. They'd just returned from loading a van with merchandise amounting to over $1 million. This new venture was on a trial basis, but so far, the numbers were good.

His phone rang. It was Arlo. "Hey."

"The garage in forty-five minutes."

"Gotcha." He didn't need to ask which one. They had just talked about Ricky earlier at their morning meeting. The guy needed cash again. The forty-five-minute agreed upon time was actually thirty, and Arlo picked him up on the way.

They stopped at the man's place of employment with the excuse of their SUV making an odd noise. Ricky came out and looked under the hood.

"I need more cash." He clutched a wrench in his hand.

"You could barely make it last time." Arlo

handled the negotiations, and it took everything Jasper had in him not to punch the mechanic in the face.

"I got things under control. Just need enough to get by until the weekend." Ricky checked a few things to make it appear he was looking the vehicle over.

"How much?" Arlo questioned.

Jasper circled around but remained within ear shot.

"Ten thousand," Ricky muttered.

It was on the tip of his tongue to ask what the cash was for, but it didn't matter. That was not their business; lending and making money was.

"You know where to go. It'll be waiting for you." Arlo stepped back. Ricky shut the hood and strutted back to the garage, his step lighter than when they'd arrived.

"You got that, Jasp?" Arlo was in a mood. Ever since he got back from Chicago, the man had been a bitch to work with. Rumor had it, the guy had the hots for Layla, Madison's half-sister.

"Yeah." Jasper was already typing the info in code into the phone. There was a pickup spot for the money, and when Richard Harrison got off work, the money would be waiting for him. "Let's go. I can't stand the sight of that guy." It wasn't like they dealt with Boy Scouts in their line of work, but some people rubbed him worse than others. The types they dealt with were usually the dregs of society, but he just couldn't abide men that hit women.

After finishing, they drove through town.

61

Tourism was starting to pick up, and the lake homes were being opened up for the season.

"Hey, pull over there." Jasper pointed.

"You see something?" Arlo did as he was told.

"Yeah." He was out of the car before it was in park. The woman sitting on the park bench had drawn his attention. It was Ricky's wife. Jasper approached slowly. Her head was down, and her hands were on her lap. "Mrs. Harrison?"

Her gaze turned up at him. The bruise on her face had darkened. "Yes?"

"Do you remember who I am?"

She nodded.

"Do you mind if I sit?" Jasper motioned toward the spot next to her.

She picked up the purse by her side and put it on her lap.

"What's your name?"

"Connie."

"I'm Jasper." He kept his distance on the bench and noticed Arlo watching him from the car.

"You're the loan sharks who came to the house." It was said as a statement and not as a question.

"I do collections," he corrected her.

"You should have come earlier in the day. He didn't have the money then." Connie let out a loud sigh.

"And you know what happens if people don't pay, right?" Did she really want him dead?

"Yes." Connie twisted his way. "I was going to leave him. Been planning for months. He found the money I'd saved up and did this." She pointed to her face. "The rest of the marks you can't see." Her voice shook.

"Has he hit you before?" The anger toward the woman's husband was growing by leaps and bounds.

"I've lived with the abuse for some time." Connie sniffled. "A person never plans on living like this, but sometimes, things happen, and you just can't escape."

"Is there anywhere you can go? Someone you can stay with?"

"I don't want temporary. I want out." She wiped away a tear.

"He just borrowed more money again." Jasper exhaled.

"I know. The guy thinks he's going to make big money betting on a game tonight. He thinks he can't lose because he's selling my car on Monday."

"You're getting a new car?" That seemed surprising.

"No, he takes everything, and I never get anything but abuse. This time, he's getting his." She met his gaze. "I made a fake profile agreeing to buy the car. If he loses the money, that'll be it. There's no one coming to pay, and we don't have any more cash."

"I see." Jasper looked at Arlo again. "Are you going to be okay? We have to make three attempts to make him pay."

"He can't pay. You only need to come once." She placed a hand on his arm.

There was nothing he'd rather do than put an end to this guy, but he worried about her safety until they could get the job done. "I'll talk to the boss."

He couldn't take things into his hands and go against the family, but he had a feeling that, in this case, Roman would agree.

"I'll see what I can do," he promised.

"Thank you." Connie winced as she smiled.

After they left the park, Jasper had Arlo stop at the flower shop.

"Now what are you doing?" Arlo complained. "I'm not your fucking chauffeur."

"Just wait here." He hurried in and came out with a bouquet of flowers and a box of chocolates.

"Seriously." His driver just shook his head. Again, the pissed-off mood for no reason.

"Yes, I am. I want this woman."

"You want all women." Arlo put the vehicle into drive.

"Not anymore." Now only a certain redhead held his attention.

"Who's the unlucky lady?" he ribbed.

"Jackie." Just saying her name made him smile. "She's my angel, and I'm determined to make her mine."

"Yeah, she seems really into you." They pulled into a fast food drive-thru.

"She is. She just doesn't know it yet." Jasper's heart ached. He'd never been in this position before, and he didn't like it one bit.

***

Jackie

Madison had ordered lunch from one of the

many great sandwich places in town. They'd discussed more of the details about the charity event while they ate. It still seemed weird that it was a bachelor auction, but after the great response they were having, it was the talk of the town.

While returning from the break room, the aroma of flowers hit her before they stepped into her office. "What the?" There, on Jackie's desk, was a gorgeous crystal vase filled with purple roses. She'd never been a flower person, but then, no one had even given her any. They were amazing. Stunning, actually. But who would have sent them?

"Wow." Madison peeked in the doorway. "Those are the most beautiful flowers I've ever seen, and I used to do weddings." She came in and lowered her nose to the petals. "And they smell wonderful."

"I think they must be for you. They probably dropped them in here by mistake." It would be amazing to be the benefactor of such a thoughtful gift.

"Why do you say that?" Her boss frowned at her.

"I, ah, I'm not dating anyone, so I'm not sure who would be sending me flowers." Jackie wrung her hands.

"I think someone wants to date you." Maddy pointed to a box that had been overshadowed by the bouquet. "You do know what purple roses stand for, don't you?"

Jackie shook her head. "I'm afraid I haven't a clue."

"It means love at first sight."

"What?" Jackie hadn't noticed it before, but she picked up the gift and looked it over. It was a small rectangular package. There was no one in love with her and certainly not at first sight. The box was wrapped in silver paper and again accented with a purple ribbon and bow.

"What's inside?" Madison sat on one of the chairs. "I'm guessing something sweet."

Jackie removed the cover and was greeted with the delicious scent of dark chocolate. "You were right." She showed her the goodies.

"Oh, my. Gunther's Chocolates. Those are my favorite."

"Want one?" Jackie held them across the desk.

Madison leaned closer but shook her head. "I'd love to, but I'd better not. Those are for you, not me."

"But who would send this? I still think it's a mistake." Jackie put the box down, took a seat, and crossed her arms in front of her chest.

"Did they send a card?" Madison stood and studied the roses.

"Ha! Never thought of that. You can tell I'm not used to getting gifts."

"Ah ha! Here it is." She handed the small card to Jackie.

"I'm afraid to look. Maybe I have a stalker." Stranger things had happened. She heard about that stuff all the time.

"Only one way to find out." Madison leaned against the doorway. "Do you want to open it in private? I can leave, if you want."

"No, that's okay." She finally opened the card. "I just nervous with all the attention." And dreaming that it was from someone that really cared about her. The note read:

Angel,

I'm looking forward to our date.

Her heartrate kicked up a notch. It was signed "Jasper." A girl could get used to this, but what did it mean? Was it all just a ploy to get her into bed and on to the next conquest?

"Well, are you going to tell me? I'm dying over here," her boss teased. "Unless you don't want to share."

Jackie handed her the card, and Madison's eyes widened. "Are you two going out?"

"He asked me, but I said no. Jasper bet me that I couldn't resist going on a date with him. Looks like he's going all out." She was briefly overcome with the romance of it all, but now it seemed like he was just playing to win the game.

"Well, I've always liked Jasper. I haven't known him long, but he's a good man. I think you should go." Madison placed the card back on the table before inhaling the fragrance again. "As they say, we don't regret the things we do; we regret the things we didn't do. Take my advice, and go out with him." With that, she left, and Jackie studied the card again. Was she attracted to him? Yes. Did she want to get involved with someone with criminal ties? Absolutely not.

Jasper's voice could be heard in the distance. She took one more whiff of the lovely blossoms and headed down the hall. The smell of hamburgers and fries increased with every step. Arlo and Jasper were chowing down on some fast food in the office the guys shared. They both looked up when she entered.

Arlo glanced her way, nodded, and returned to eating. She didn't know him well, but he seemed to be a sour puss. Jasper winked and popped a fry into his mouth. Her eyes lingered on his mouth before she dragged them away. His jaw was lightly covered with sexy stubble and her knees felt weak.

Arlo gathered his food wrappers and stood up. "I'm losing my appetite. See you later."

"Yeah, sure." Jasper frowned at the man who left, but when he looked her way, his mouth turned into a smile. "I must say, I prefer your company to his any day. Have a seat." He pulled a chair out for her.

"I can't stay." But she sat down anyway. "Is he all right? I don't think I've ever seen him in a good mood."

Jasper shrugged. "He's interested in a woman he can't have. Good thing I don't have that problem." He winked, and it warmed her from inside out, even though it shouldn't.

"About that…" she started.

"Do you like the flowers?" He seemed so eager to please her.

"Who wouldn't? They're the most beautiful ones I've ever seen."

"Just like the person I gave them to." He brushed her fingers with hers. They were slippery from the fries, but she didn't mind.

"And the candy," Jackie added.

"Sweets for the sweet." The guy didn't give up, and it was going to get harder and harder to say no.

"Jasper. I really appreciate them, but I'm still not going to go out with you."

"And why not?" He tilted his head.

"I don't know how to put this, but it needs to be said." Although she really didn't want to.

The cocky expression on his face softened, making him even more attractive. "Go on."

"I know I shouldn't be working here feeling this way, but I did some searching online. Madison's husband is the son of a Chicago Mafia boss. He's involved in crime. If you work for him, that means you are also. I don't want any trouble." There, she said it. It wasn't that she didn't find him attractive, Lord knew she did, but getting involved was crossing into dangerous territory.

"You aren't in any danger. From what I heard, Maddy wanted nothing to do with Roman when they met, but he won her over anyway. They love each other, and from what I've seen, they are very happy. Despite what you think you know about me, I want that kind of a relationship also."

Jackie stood up. "You're right. I don't know you, but you can't have that kind of relationship with me." Pain crossed his face as if he'd been stuck. As much as it hurt to say it, it had to be said. There was no future for them. He was charming, drop dead gorgeous, and would probably give her the best sex of her life, but she was just a simple girl. One that didn't want her heart broken by a handsome gangster.

Chapter Seven

Jasper

It was Monday, and his bad temper had started to match Arlo's. They both needed to get laid, but not just any woman would do. The weekend had dragged. He'd hoped to run into Jackie but didn't catch sight of her anywhere. It was on the tip of his tongue to ask the tech guys to find her, but that bordered on creepy.

He'd felt like a hermit staying inside, so he'd called Dominic and Stephanie to go for a run along the lake on Saturday. Oddly enough, later in the day, Arlo invited him over to his place to watch a movie Saturday night. They'd enjoyed some booze, pizza, and John Wick flicks, while wishing they were with someone of the opposite sex.

Sunday, he'd slept in and lingered in the Java Shop like a lovesick teenager, hoping Jackie would drop in. There'd been several ladies who stopped to say "hi," but he hadn't encouraged them to stay longer. At least he had Madison's assurance that the lady in question would be betting on him at the bachelor auction and winning.

In the afternoon, he'd visited his grandfather, Frankie. The man was getting up in years, and Jasper had found a nice place in Genoa for him to live. So far, things were going well, and he was adjusting nicely to the smaller city after living in Chicago for such a long time. Even that didn't improve Jasper's frame of mind.

Finally, Sunday evening had rolled around. The only thing keeping him sane was the fact he'd get to see his Angel Monday and hopefully send Richard Harrison to hell.

It felt great to be back at work, and he'd been with Roman most of the day. They had to deliver some of the bigger high-end merchandise to their new owners. For the most part, Jasper enjoyed the variety of things he got to do in Genoa. Roman was an underboss, and his father was the boss, but they kept their businesses separate, unless his father needed help.

It was unheard off for Roman to do business that way, but he said it was the new age of doing things.

Arlo and Jasper were both made men and had taken the oath. They were in it for life. There was no getting out, and neither would ever dream of it. Jasper's father had been a capo before being killed, and his father, Frankie, was in the family as well. Only age and health had caused him to retire.

They were done around three. Roman left with Oscar, and Jasper met Arlo in town. Dom had stayed all day at the winery. He was working on some of the construction, so that was a nice change of pace for the guy.

"Let's go visit Ricky a little after five. He'll be alone then." Arlo took a final sip of coffee and tossed it in a nearby trash can. "What did you find out from the boss?"

"I talked to Roman, and he's okay with offing the piece of shit today." Jasper couldn't wait to get rid of the guy fast enough. He didn't want the risk of Ricky hurting his wife, if the man figured out that she'd set him up.

"Good, finally a little excitement." He rubbed his hands together. "Who's with Maddy, if Dom's got to get rid of the body?"

"We're not getting rid of the body." Jasper and he had just left the donut shop and were now walking to Arlo's SUV.

"Why not?" He flipped his sunglasses off his head and onto his nose.

"Can't collect life insurance if there's no body. I had the techies check. The only policy on him is through his work. If we make it look like an accident, Connie will get some money for having to put up with that asshole."

Arlo just nodded and got in the car. "Then let's do it."

They waited down the road until the last car left the garage where Richard worked. Then Arlo parked the vehicle behind the building, in case someone chose to drive by.

Ricky was changing the oil on a Jeep when they came in the back door.

Jasper strolled up to the vehicle, while Arlo stayed back. They didn't want to panic the guy any more than they probably were. Jumpy people made things messy and complicated, and that was more work than it was worth. They looked out of place as it was. Two guys in suits in a greasy garage. The smell of oil and rubber lingered in the air.

"Working late so you can earn some extra money, or do you have it for us now?"

Rick jumped. He dropped the wrench in his hand, and it clinked on the concrete floor. "Oh, hi, fellas. I was just going to call." He wiped his hands on his coveralls.

"Yeah, well. Just hand over the money," Jasper barked, hoping he wouldn't have it as Connie suggested.

"That's why I was going to phone. I need more time." The guy shook like a leaf. "I was going to save you the trip."

"Always thinking of others, aren't you?" Arlo stepped out in view, and Jasper approached Ricky slowly. "Well, you've run out of time."

"What do you mean?" Ricky glanced from one man to the other. "I get three visits."

"This is your third visit," Jasper stressed. "You didn't have the money the last time."

Ricky's mouth dropped open. "What the fuck? I gave it to you. You came to my house. Connie can vouch for me."

"The cash you gave me belonged to someone else. You can't pay with stolen money."

"What the hell are you talking about?" The man reached for a rag and wiped his hands.

"That belonged to your wife." Jasper smirked.

Ricky shook his head. "Are you shitting me?

73

We're married. Her money is my money."

"Not when you gamble it all away and she has to scrape by. It's not your money when she has to hide it so she can get away before you beat her again." Jasper approached, and Ricky took a step back until he bumped into a table.

"You believe her?" he sputtered.

"I do, and this will be your last visit." Jasper took a deep breath. He'd enjoy getting rid of this piece of shit.

"You can't do this. That bitch is lying!" Ricky yelled.

"Bruises don't lie. That's why we have to make your death look like an accident." Jasper glanced toward Arlo, who was now circling around to Ricky's side. "She can collect the insurance money from your death."

"Jesus." There was a green tinge to Ricky's face.

"He can't help you now." Arlo pulled a pair of leather gloves out of his pockets and slipped them on.

"Come on." Ricky appeared on the verge of bolting. "Give me a break. I'll disappear. She'll never see me again. You'll never see me again."

"No, it's time to die." Jasper smiled. This guy had it coming.

"Well, if you think I'm going to make this easy for you, you got another thing coming." Ricky reached for the wrench he had dropped and started waving it around.

Jasper pulled a taser from his pocket and hit the button. Ricky dropped to the floor like a bug that ran into a zapper. "Yeah, good luck with that."

Arlo now stood next to him. "What should we do with him?" He glanced around the garage. "Run his arm through a saw and have him bleed to death?"

"It's a garage, not a lumber yard." He sneered. "Does anything look like it could catch on fire or explode?"

"What do I know? I drive cars. Changing the oil and the occasional tire change is the extent of my mechanical abilities." Arlo was as out of place here as he was.

They both explored around the building, but nothing really stood out. "Where's Dominic when you need him? He good at staging shit like this."

"Probably done for the day."

Ricky moaned and struggled to his knees. Arlo kicked him in the ribs, and the man fell over. "Hey, no bruises." Jasper scolded before walking over and kicking him between the legs. Richard let out a blood-curdling scream.

"A boot to the balls. Hurts like hell and leaves no marks." Jasper raised an eyebrow toward Arlo.

"You've been watching too much CSI. It's fucking with your head and making you a smartass," Arlo teased.

"You can't be too careful. These days, cops can find a nose hair and track down a killer." Jasper approached a full-sized pickup truck. "You really have to stay on top of that stuff. I once heard of a case where, during the interrogation, the cops told a guy this story about how a person sheds a ton of skin cells every day, and they found some of his at the crime scene. They hadn't, but the guy was so freaked out, he confessed to everything."

75

"I miss the old days when you could just shoot a guy in the head, chop him up into pieces, and toss the rest in the lake. Nowadays, if you did that and got caught, they'd probably tag on extra time for illegal dumping or some other EPA bullshit."

"True." Jasper eyed the truck again. "Is this on a lift?"

"Looks like it." Arlo circled to the back.

"Find the button to raise it." They both searched, until Arlo found it on a nearby post.

Ricky groaned and started to crawl away. Jasper tried the taser again, but the charge was spent.

"Here, try this." Arlo handed him a long rod with a red handle and two prods on the one end.

"Cattle prod." He nodded toward Arlo. "Good choice." Jasper gave the man on the floor another jolt.

"Maybe we could just crank it up and give him a heart attack?"

Jasper frowned. "If only it were that easy. We don't have that much time." He motioned to the truck. "Let's raise that and drop it on him."

"I like that idea." Ricky whimpered and rolled onto his side. Between the voltage and the hits, he wasn't in the best shape to put up much of any disagreement.

Arlo pressed the button and raised the truck up a couple of feet. They grabbed the bully and placed him under the front tire.

"Any last words, dumbass?" Jasper shook the man.

Ricky's eyes rolled around in his head. He would probably pass out soon from the stress alone, but he managed to speak. "Go to hell, and tell Connie that too."

The fucker was getting the easy way out. Jasper would love nothing better than to make him pay in long and agonizing misery for hurting his wife.

"She won't be going there, but you sure will." Jasper gave Arlo the thumbs up to hit the switch, and the wheels lowered onto Ricki's chest. "Punch a hole in the hydraulics." Arlo did as told, and a hiss echoed from the hose as the truck lurched to the ground. Ricky made one last wheezing sound, probably from all the air exiting his lungs as his chest was crushed.

Jasper squatted down to make sure the man was dead. "I think we're done." Arlo stood beside him, staring at the dead man. "You want to get a drink?" Jasper rose.

"You don't have a date? What, your flowers didn't do the trick?" Arlo teased as they made sure everything was in its place and the shop looked like they'd never been there. Well, except for the guy under the truck tires.

"I'm working on it." They exited the back door and strolled toward their vehicle. It was a nice night and still pretty warm out. "I didn't see her all day, but I sent a little gift to her, anyway."

"Didn't she used to be a reporter?" Arlo hit the key fob and unlocked the doors. "Those people are pretty nosy. What if she's just using this job to snoop around?"

"She quit the paper and seems to like working with Madison. The woman's smart and has to know what she's doing. Madison wouldn't have hired her if she were a threat."

"Yeah, she doesn't want to go out with you, so the girl must be smart." Arlo laughed.

"Hey, before I'm done, Jackie will be begging me to marry her." Jasper eased into the seat.

"You? Married? Tell me another one." Arlo started the car.

"Hey, a guy's got to bite the bullet sometime." Marriage? Where had that come from? "But right now, I'd be happy with a date. How about you? Rumor has it there's something between you and Madison's sister."

"Half-sister. And no, there's nothing going on between Layla and me." They pulled out cautiously from behind the building, but there were no cars anywhere in sight.

"But you'd like there to be?" Jasper asked.

"Who wouldn't? She's the most beautiful woman I've ever seen."

Jasper nudged him in the arm. "Now I know you have the hots for her because guys always think the one you love is the most beautiful."

"Little good that will do me," Arlo cursed. "She's the sister-in-law to my boss, and a soldier never ends up with the queen." The man's voice dropped.

"Well, technically, she's not a queen. More of a princess, since her father is a don," Jasper corrected.

"Either way, I don't have a chance in hell."

They spent the rest of the trip in silence before Arlo dropped him off at his place. Arlo may have given up on going after the woman he wanted, but that was something Jasper would never do. Jackie would be his. She just didn't realize it yet.

Chapter Eight

Jackie

The past week had flown by. Planning an event in less than seven days was quite the undertaking. Besides the flyers around town, they'd also sent out private invitations. Tickets had sold out in a flash. Since they would be working late, Madison had given her the morning off, and Jackie was now savoring her caramel mocha at the Java Shop.

Her fingers touched the necklace around her neck. It had been waiting for her when she arrived this morning. As were other gifts that arrived each day from a certain guy who always caused her heart to beat faster whenever he was nearby. They always arrived in a white bag or box and were accented with a purple bow or ribbon. It was the last thing she should be wearing, but screw it. She loved it. The Brighton necklace with the large Swarovski pendant felt warm on her chest. Jasper hadn't been around much this week, but every day, he'd sent a present, sometimes two. Most were more on the thoughtful than high-end price, which helped with the guilt of keeping them.

A fruit basket, a teddy bear, gift certificate to a spa, perfume, the latest bestselling romance novel, and today was the necklace. At first, she tried to give them back when he was there, but the man refused. He said they were gifts and non-returnable. Jasper didn't ask her out anymore, either, which was odd. Did he think she'd just give in because he was trying to buy her affections?

It was getting harder and harder to resist the man. Gifts were something other girls always received, not her. Was it a crime that she wanted to enjoy the attention for however long it lasted? Jackie knew the necklace was pricey. It was a brand she'd always admired from afar but had never been able to afford. He either had great taste or could read her mind. The man also seemed to be giving her space. Almost like he knew she didn't like being pressured but needed to weigh her options in her head first. It was working. Not only was she attracted to him physically, but he was starting to win her over with his patience. The man was an obvious charmer, but playboys never impressed her.

"Hey, long time no see." It was her former boss from the paper.

"Hi, Bruce." Jackie pushed the chair opposite her out with her foot. "Have a seat."

"Thanks, but only for a minute." He set his Genoa Java cup on the table and sat down. "I'm on my way to a big story."

"Really? Here?" She rolled her eyes. "Did someone catch a new record large fish?"

"No, something even bigger." Bruce took a sip of coffee and seemed to enjoy dragging out the suspense. "There's been a robbery."

"What?" That was news. "A bank robbery?"

"No, Rodney Studd had a Picasso stolen." Bruce was practically giddy and bounced in his seat. "Right off the wall of his office."

"Rodney Studd? The rockstar?" Jackie frowned and picked up her pen. "That seems odd."

"What? That it was stolen or that he had a Picasso?"

"Both, actually. Who would take that, and how'd they get in? Things like that just don't happen around here." Or at least when she worked at the Globe they didn't.

"I know. Rumor has it the guy's up to his hair extensions in debt, and off the record, police said nothing showed up on the security tapes." He leaned back in his chair. "I'm thinking insurance fraud."

"Hmm. So we don't have a cat burglar out and about?" That would've been more exciting.

"At this point in time, no, but we can always hope." Bruce lowered his voice. "I mean to say, it would make for more sales for the paper, but I'd never want a criminal on the loose."

"That's for sure." She liked living in a safe town.

"How's the new job going?"

"Good. I'm learning a lot. Tonight's the big charity auction." Hopefully, it'd go well. She'd lined up several bachelors, and various stores in town, including the Java Shop, were donating prizes. "I hope the Globe is going to cover it."

"Wouldn't miss it."

"Great. I'll see you there." Jackie finished her coffee and got to her feet. "I better get going. I've got a lot to do before the event."

"See you later." Bruce grabbed his cup and headed out the door.

Jackie had been to Firenza before. One of her first jobs at the paper had been to cover the Snowflake Ball that was held there every fall, but this was different. This time, it was her job to make sure everything fell into place. Luckily, Madison was an expert at it.

All the tables had been decorated with black tablecloths and red napkins. Flowers were everywhere, also matching the color scheme of black, red, and green. There was a buffet of appetizers and fire-roasted pizzas. Attendees were able to try a flight of wines, and all the ladies would also receive a gift bag full of a variety of goodies donated by different businesses in town.

Madison stood at the entrance, welcoming people inside, while Jackie handed them their gift bags. A few even contained gift cards and other extra prizes.

"Maddy." The tall woman in the high heels Jackie had seen at the coffee shop that morning long ago gave her boss a big hug. "This is so exciting. Congrats on the new enterprise."

"Thank you, and thanks for coming." Madison had dressed in a beautiful, strapless, white and red floral dress. The woman had designed it and made it herself. Was there anything she couldn't do? "This is my assistant, Jackie. She helped pull all this together. Jackie, this is my sister-in-law, Valentina."

"It's nice to meet you." Jackie shook her hand and smiled. "I think I met your husband at the police station when I was handing out flyers."

"You did. He was glad he was married so he had a reason to say no." She winked. "But he couldn't say no to babysitting so I could come support you tonight."

"That's wonderful." Madison smiled.

"So, what charity did you pick?" Valentina accepted the gift bag and peeked inside.

"In order to get the guys from the fire station to join in, we had to agree to donate the money to some new safety equipment." The majority of the fire departments in Wisconsin were volunteer only, so they often held fundraisers to earn money and pay for expenses.

"Well, that's a great cause. Since I won't be bidding on any bachelors, be sure to remind me to write a check before I go."

"Will do." Madison kissed her cheeks. "And thanks for everything. Would you mind helping me meet guests while Jackie keeps any eye on the food and the guests in the main room?"

"Of course. I'd love to." Valentina was also stunningly dressed from her diamond earrings to the red-soled shoes.

Jackie nodded at Val as she left the two and strolled into the banquet room. Since being hired, Jackie had done some research on the Caponelli family. The last thing she thought she'd be doing since leaving the paper was spending more time at the computer investigating people, but that's exactly what was happening.

Roman was the only son of the head of the Caponelli crime family, and Valentina was his sister. She was a very accomplished lawyer, but since her marriage and their new baby girl, she'd cut back on the legal practice. Her husband, Ryan, was an unlikely suitor, being that he was a local police officer. From Jackie's research, it seemed that Roman was trying to make this branch of the family legit with the restaurant, winery, and other ventures, but appearances could often be deceiving. He could be laundering money through them, for all she knew.

While doing her search, other names had popped up online. Arlo, Dominic, and Jasper all had minor police records, and except for Arlo, no one had served any prison time. Obviously, they had a top-notch lawyer on the payroll. Jackie had called in a favor to a friend, Cory, at the old paper in Chicago, for more info. Cory knew someone in records at the police station, so Jackie hoped to find out further info about the three of them. If she was going to be working around these people, she needed to know what she was dealing with.

The winery seemed safe, and hopefully, it was, but a girl couldn't be too careful. And then there was Jasper. The guy had "bad boy" written all over him, yet ladies fell for him in droves. The man was the hottest thing in a three-piece suit, but that was not the sort of guy she needed. What kind did she need, for that matter? Certainly not one with a record. Her father had set the standard high, and no one would ever likely come close. But, still, temptation was a hard drug to turn down.

They'd interacted several times at work. It was hard not to, but what did he really do? His job there was to do...what? Security? What was there to watch over there? She was probably the only woman in town he hadn't been out with, and that seemed to bother her more than anything. Jackie didn't want to admit she wanted him, but she didn't want anyone else to, either.

Jackie looked down at the simple shoes on her feet. Valentina's had been designer, and Madison's probably weren't cheap, either. Guys didn't care about shoes; they just wanted a cute girl on their arm. But she'd never been lucky in that department. Men always seemed to want the petite blondes and not the tall redheads. Jackie frowned. She was no beauty queen, but still, she wasn't chopped liver, either. The man in her life should be honorable, not a criminal. Why was she even thinking about Jasper again? He was bad news and the last person in the world she needed to be associated with.

But still...

Ugh.

It was time to get back to work and not think about anything else.

After making sure all the wine was still free flowing and every guest had a glass in their hand, she double checked the buffet area. Everything looked amazing. After that, she ushered guests to their tables. The auction was about to start. Jackie stood along the wall to be ready in case anyone needed anything that the servers missed. Unfortunately, as hard as she tried, Jackie couldn't get Jasper out of her mind. Damn that man for his wonderful gifts and tempting bet.

"Is everything all right?" Madison touched her elbow.

"Oh, yes. Sorry. I was day dreaming."

"You looked sad." Maddy titled her head. "Is everything okay? I haven't been working you too hard, have I?"

"Oh, no. Nothing like that." She blushed.

"Are you sure?"

"Yes. Everything's fine."

"Well, you've done a great job with this, and I really appreciate all your hard work." She glanced at her phone. "It's almost time."

"What do you want me to do now?" Jackie had done all the planning and set up, but they hadn't talked about what she was supposed to do once the auction started.

"Take a seat at our table and enjoy yourself. Stephanie is lining up the guys, so rest your feet. You don't have anything to do until it's time to clean up for that night."

"Great. Sounds like a plan." It would be nice to sit down. Her feet did ache.

Their reserved table was toward the side. Valentina was already seated there, chatting on her phone. From the big smile on her face and the giggling on the phone, it was obvious she was talking to her husband and daughter.

"Attention, everyone." Jackie turned toward the stage. Madison had taken the microphone. "I would like to welcome you ladies here tonight on behalf of Bella Luna Wines. I hope you enjoyed the wine and food. There are two additional wine samples at every setting, chocolate samples, and some delicious cake from the Java Shop. If you need any more, the servers with gladly get that for you."

She went on to describe the wines and to share a bit about their new winery. Madison also talked about the charity and that all money raised would be going to Genoa's volunteer fire department.

When she asked for a show of hands for those that wanted more to drink, every hand in the audience went up. That was a great sign. Also, the more they drank, the more they would spend. Madison introduced a couple more speakers. Local women, who shared a bit about their businesses and also gave a few prizes from their businesses. One owned a spa, and the other owned a chocolate shop. Jackie made a note to visit the candy store. The samples in the gift bag were to die for. That must have been where Jasper bought the sweets he'd given her.

"And, lastly, but not leastly. Leastly? Is that even a word?" she joked. "How about, last but not least, we have our bachelor auction. These nice gentlemen, all single of course, have agreed to help out. Get out your wallets, ladies. Bid the highest, and you will win a date night dinner at Firenza and a bottle of wine with your bachelor."

The ladies all cheered and whistled.

Valentina said goodnight to her loved ones and tucked her cell into her purse.

Madison handed the microphone over to a local realtor, Sandy Asher. The woman also held auctions, and Sandy had the perfect voice for it too, as she introduced the first bachelor to walk down the runway.

"I can't believe that Roman agreed to this." Valentina shook her head.

"Believe me, he wasn't happy about it, but when I reminded him that his nickname used to be Romeo, he didn't say any more." Madison reached for her wine glass. "He refused to let me borrow any of the men, though."

"I thought Jasper was doing it," Jackie spoke up.

"Yes, he is, but not any of others." Madison arched her eyebrow. "Are you going to bid on him?"

"What? Ah, no. Of course not." This time Jackie reached for the wine. Was it okay to drink on the job?

"Why not?" Both women gawked at her.

"Well, look at what they're bidding." They all looked toward the stage, where the bidding for the first guy was already up to one thousand dollars. "That's more than my rent."

"So you're saying you'd bid on Jasper if you had that kind of money?" Her boss was clearly teasing, but Jackie didn't know how to answer.

"Sorry to interrupt, but Madison, can I have a word with you?" It was the spa lady wanting to offer a couple's massage as another door prize. It also saved her from answering that question. Would she bid on Jasper if she could?

The practical side in her said no, but the adventurous girl in her said yes, yes, yes.

Chapter Nine

Jackie

The lineup of guys was pretty impressive, but none really caught her eye like Jasper. Jackie was already comparing him to other men. That wasn't a good sign. It clearly meant she had fallen under his spell. There were others who were tall, dark, and handsome, but it was his all-knowing eyes that always seemed to see right through her and cause that little spark to ignite. And then there was that amazing hair too. How much time had she already spent imagining what it would feel like to run her fingers through the thick strands?

Reaching for a napkin, she used it as a fan.

"I know, right? The guys are hot and really putting on a show." Valentina raised her glass. "Why didn't they have this when I was single?"

"Or me?" Madison added as she returned to her seat. "You really need to raise your hand and get in there, Jackie."

Jackie just sat there and smiled. The ladies doing

the bidding definitely had more money in their bank accounts than she'd ever had or could dream to have.

There were twenty guys on the roster, and after two hours, they were up to number nineteen. Not knowing the listing, Jackie had no idea when Jasper might pop up on the runway, but they had obviously saved the best for last. Her stomach was in knots. Just because she wasn't sure of her feelings for him didn't mean she wanted someone else to have him, either. Each guy seemed to be hotter than the last. Mr. Nineteen did a little dance as he strutted down the stage. He was dressed like a cowboy, complete with a hat, jeans, and boots. They ladies hooted and hollered. Glancing around the room, everyone seemed to be having a great time.

The bidding amount rose with each man. The cowboy was close to $5,000.00 already. It was amazing. Either the women in this town were very generous to charity, or they were desperate for a date. Madison squealed when the final bid hit $7,550.00. The man jumped off the stage and gave the winner some flowers and a kiss on the cheek.

"This is crazy." Valentina clapped along with the crowd. "This is really going to help get the equipment the fire department needs. You could do this every year for a different charity. Just think of all the good that would do!"

"I know. Wouldn't that be awesome?" Madison glowed.

"Ladies, we have one more handsome guy hoping to win your heart." The auctioneer drew their attention back to the stage. *Earned It* from the

Fifty Shades of Grey soundtrack began to play. That song oozed sex appeal, and so did the man who walked out onto the stage. It was Jasper. He flashed that breathtaking smile, and the ladies ate it up like candy.

Usually, he wore three-piece suits, but tonight, he'd shed the jacket. Dressed in black pinstripe pants, a vest, and a burgundy shirt, Jasper was his usual stylish self. Tonight, he wore no tie, and the casual look made him even more appealing. The auctioneer introduced him as Jasper Lencioni, local business man, but left out the part about what kind of business he was in.

Sandy started the first bid at a thousand dollars, and several hands went up. Jasper strolled down the runway like he owned it, and he did. As always, he had flawless hair. It was as if he'd run his fingers through it and the locks just magically fell into place.

When he stopped at the end and turned around, her mouth dropped open. How had she never noticed his firm butt before? The guy was too perfect to be true. Jasper spotted their table and winked her way.

It must have been all the wine, right? Jackie's cheeks flamed. God, she wanted him. They always said competition was good. Well, right now, it was pissing her off. Tonight, someone else would win the guy that intrigued her so.

"Come on, Jackie. I know you like him, and he likes you." Madison nudged her with her elbow.

"Even if I did, I don't have that kind of cash." Jackie tried to brush off the comment.

"So you would go out with him if you could?" Her boss was obviously trying to play matchmaker.

"Maybe." She almost said yes, but she still held back. The man was a mystery to her. A mystery with a questionable background.

The bidding hit $9,000.00, and several disappointed women shook their heads and dropped their hands.

"Do I hear $10,000.00?" the auctioneer asked.

"Oh my goodness." Valentina squealed, but Jackie just wanted it to be over. She was already jealous of whoever the winner would be.

"Do I hear $10,000.00?" the woman with the mic asked again.

"Jackie?" Maddy touched her forearm. "I think you have a huge rip in your blouse."

"What?" That's all she needed. To look like a hot mess while Jasper went to some wealthy woman dressed to the nines. "Where? I can't believe this." Her fingers felt around, but she couldn't feel anything out of place.

"On your side, under your arm." Madison lifted Jackie's arm in the air.

"Are you sure? I still don't see anything." Maybe she wasn't the only one who'd had too much drink. Madison was seeing things that weren't there. Good thing the woman had a driver because she shouldn't be behind the wheel.

"Sold." All eyes turned to the stage, where the auctioneer pointed to their table. "Sold to the pretty redhead at table five."

"What?" Jackie's mouth dropped open, and she lowered her arm. "Oh. My. God."

"Congrats, you won Jasper." Valentina clapped her hands.

"I didn't! I was just looking, looking..." She turned to face Madison, who at least had the decency to look embarrassed. "You set me up."

"I'm sorry, but I just think you two would be great together." At least she admitted it.

"For $10,000.00?" A lump lodged in her throat. Where would she come up with that kind of money? This went against everything that should be appropriate for a working relationship.

"Don't worry about that. The business will pay. It's a donation. Look, you have to be there anyway for work. Would it be so bad to just sit down and share a meal with him for an hour?"

Jasper arrived at their table, a huge grin on his face and a bouquet of red roses in his arms. He handed her the flowers and gave her a kiss on the cheek, something that the other bachelors had also done for the ones that'd bid the most. But this seemed personal. Several of the ladies who were nearby sighed. "See you tomorrow night for our date." He winked and flashed a panty-melting smile. Her cheek flushed and she was too shocked to respond. Jasper said his goodnights to the others at their table and walked backstage as Sandy finished up the program for the night.

Jackie drew the flowers closer and inhaled the fragrance. The guy did know how to pick flowers.

"Well? Am I forgiven?" Madison fidgeted in her chair.

"I should be furious, but I'm not. I know you mean well." Jackie's gaze met Valentina's. She had that hopeful demeanor of someone who was in love and wanted others to be also.

"But?" Madison frowned.

"No buts. I'll do it." Her companions visibly relaxed. "It's not everyday that someone pays $10,000.00 for you to go on a date." Jackie interlocked her fingers and placed them on the table. "That said, I'll be working, so don't expect us to be a couple by the end of the evening."

"No, no. I just wanted to do something nice for you," her boss admitted.

"So you bought me a date? Do I come across that desperate?" Maybe she did need to get out more, if it was the case.

"No, of course not, but I know Jasper really likes you. He's a good guy, and I think you two will be a good match."

"We'll see." Jackie stood up. "I'd better get back to work."

The attendees stayed around for another hour or so. Most of the bachelors seemed to want to start their dates early and ended up hanging out with the one who'd won them. Well, except for Jasper. He'd left the premises, which both puzzled and disappointed her.

Jackie was exhausted as she finished packing things up for the evening. At least most of the wine was gone. Those bottles were heavy. Her tasks mostly included putting away decorations and jotting down notes for items that needed to be reordered for future events.

"Anyone want to come to my house for a cocktail?" There were shadows under Madison's eyes, but she still was up for celebrating.

"I'm in." Valentina raised her hand. "As long as Ryan's watching the baby, I'm taking advantage of it."

"Jackie, how about you? Want to celebrate being the big winner?" Her boss wasn't giving up.

"Yes, come on. We haven't had a chance to get to know each other yet." Valentina's phone buzzed, and she grinned at the photo that popped up.

"That would be nice, but I'd love a raincheck. I'm pretty tired. I also have to rest up for my big date tomorrow." She rolled her eyes. "I don't think he's as interested as you say, or he wouldn't have left so early."

"He was supposed to be working tonight, so he only had a few hours off." Madison looped her purse over her shoulder.

"Well, they're done now with whatever they were doing because they're all at my house," Valentina shared.

"Really? Is there something we need to be concerned about?" Madison oohed and aahed when Val showed her the phone.

"Not that I know of. Looks like they're just hanging out." Valentina passed her cell to Jackie, and her heart thawed for the hottest man in Genoa. It was a picture of Jasper holding a smiling baby in his arms.

***

Jasper

Despite having finally gotten a date set up with the girl he wanted, his days of being a runway bachelor were over. After his bit was done, Jasper drove to Valentina and Ryan's house. Their stunning mansion was conveniently located next door to Roman and Madison's home.

Roman, Arlo, Dominic, and, of course, Ryan were already there. They'd a meeting with the Mayhem biker club earlier tonight but, for some unknown reason, were now at a cop's house. A cop who had married into the family. The Mayhem club had increased their order for guns, and the Caponellis were their main supplier—something Ryan didn't need to know anything about.

"Hey." Ryan opened the door and invited him in. As he trailed him to the den, Jasper could already hear the guys hanging out, drinking beers and laughing.

"Hi, Jasper. How'd the auction go?" Arlo smirked as he entered the room.

"Great." Jasper took a drink of the beer Ryan handed him and set it on a nearby table. "Jackie won me, which means I won her."

"Seriously?" Dominic raised an eyebrow. "They should pay the girl to go out with an ugly mug like you."

"Ha ha." He knew Dom was kidding. "In a way we did."

"You must really like this woman." Ryan joined in the ribbing.

"I do, and I had a little help from Maddy." He

bent over and picked up Isabella. "Hi, little lady."

"I don't even want to know." Roman shook his head.

"How did the drop off go?" Jasper took a seat and balanced the baby on his knee.

"Now, that, I don't want to know." Ryan put his hands up.

"Everything's good." Roman nodded to his brother-in-law before turning his attention to the others in the room. "But something happened, and Ryan wanted to wait until you got here to talk about it."

"Oh, yeah." Jasper smiled as Ryan took his picture with his daughter. She had all the guys wrapped around her little fingers. Isabella was a beautiful baby with dark hair and bright blue eyes.

"Yeah, and it's not good." The mood in the room dimmed, and Jasper held the girl in his arms a little tighter. "A woman was found along the road last night. We've held it from the news for as long as we could, but it'll be out in the morning."

"What happened? And who is she?

"And why the secrecy?" Roman leaned forward and rested his elbows on his knees.

"The woman was raped and tortured brutally. Whoever did this left her for dead, but fortunately, she was found by a doctor on his way home from work. He was able to keep her alive until the ambulance arrived. We hoped she'd wake up enough to give us the details of who did this, but she's still unconscious. If it hit the news too early, the guy might leave town, maybe already has, but we want to get him first." Ryan exhaled. His face was pale. "It was the worst I've ever seen. This guy's a fucking monster." As an officer of the law, he'd been at several crime scenes, so if Ryan said this was bad, it was.

"What can we do to help?" Arlo spoke up.

"I'm not sure right now," Ryan admitted. "But I'm hoping you might know something."

"What makes you think that?" Roman leaned back in his chair.

"The woman has several tattoos—Russian tattoos. One of the other guys on the force used to work in Chicago. He recognized one as a bratva tattoo. Thinks that girl may have worked in one of their brothels."

Jasper's gaze met Arlo's. Why would they have left one of their girls here? The Bratva had been breaching their territories in Chicago. Was this a sign that they were hitting here next? But why hurt one of their girls? None of it made any sense.

"Just keep an eye out for anything out of the ordinary, and keep your loved ones close to home," Ryan warned.

"How's the woman doing now?" Jasper couldn't imagine what the poor girl and her family, if they even knew where she was, must be going through.

"Not good. I never thought I would say this, but if you come across the bastard that did this," Ryan took a deep breath, "I don't want to know about it, and I don't care how you do it, but take him out."

Chapter Ten

Jackie

Thank God it was Friday. The week had been busy and long, and normally, she'd be counting down the hours to closing time, but today was different.

The dinner for the winners of the charity auction was tonight. It was the night of her date with Jasper. As much as she tried to ignore him, it was like trying to block a mountain from her view. It just wasn't happening.

Butterflies floated across her stomach, and that hadn't happened in a long time, maybe never. The guy hadn't been at work all day, and she still had no clue about what he really did there. The gist of it was that someone had to be around all the time to look after Madison. After trying to engage Dominic in conversation, he'd let it slip that the reason Maddy had a bodyguard was because she was a target. Any harm to her would be a direct hit to Roman's heart.

Dominic worked most of the day installing an iron railing along the front of the building. The man was a master at it and could probably be paid a hefty rate for his craftsmanship. When she complimented him on it, he just brushed it off and went back to work.

Madison advised her to leave work early and get dressed up for the evening. They both had to be there a few hours before it started to supervise the decorating and finals details. She'd even used one of the gift cards Jasper had given her to get her hair done for the party.

Jackie drove to Firenza and parked toward the back of the lot. As she walked to the building, the boats on the lake could be seen floating by in the background. The late afternoon sun warmed her skin, and she stopped for a moment to take in the gorgeous day. Wisconsin winters could be brutal. Taking a moment to absorb the blessings of a perfect summer day was something to cherish, and remember, when the temps dropped below zero again.

Having not attended many parties, her dress wardrobe was sorely lacking. Thankfully, Madison had lent her a simple, black, knee-length sheath dress. It fit like a glove and went perfectly with the earrings Jasper gave her and the stunning matching bracelet that showed up today. Again, shame kicked in that she should return them, but was it so bad that she didn't?

Flats were on her feet, and her heels were in her hands. Later, before the guests started to arrive, that would change. One of the family's SUVs was parked out front. Funny how she was already referring to them as "the family."

Jackie walked in the front entrance and quickly found Madison in the dining room. The woman had energy to burn and obviously enjoyed what she was doing.

"Hey, Jackie." Madison pushed a chair closer to a table. "Everything is pretty well set, but if you can make sure to put the flower arrangements around, that would be great."

Flowers. It looked like there was a wedding taking place. The arrangements matched the colors of the winery with their reds, whites, and greens. Each table would have a small bouquet that would go home with the lady.

"Oh, here is the seating chart, and the tray over there has the place cards on it." She pointed in the direction of the tray and name plates.

It didn't take long before Jackie came across the ones with Jasper and her names on them. Shit just got real, and it hadn't dawned on her until now how similar their names were. They could have monogramed everything.

Whoa! Back up, girl. Don't send out the invitations yet.

It was just a date. Like she expected all along, he'd probably be bored with her now that she'd said yes. What was it about guys loving the chase more than the catch? The journey being more fun than getting to the final destination.

Their assigned table was by the window and offered a great view of the lake. Each table would have the small floral bouquets on them, but a few had other things. Something that one of the attendees or both had requested. Their table had purple flowers. Jasper sure seemed to like purple. When she had time, she'd have to look up the meaning behind them. Maddy said it meant love at first sight, but he surely didn't feel that way about her.

As soon as the clock hit six, the guests started to arrive. Her black pumps pinched her toes after wearing them for only two minutes, but they did make her legs look long as she stood next to Madison and greeted their guests. A lot of the bachelors were already there, and several introduced themselves to their dates before escorting them around the room or out to view the lake. The first hour, waiters worked the room, carrying trays of champagne and hors d'oeuvres.

Jackie snagged a flute of the bubbly as one of the servers walked by, and she peeked at her watch. It was nearing seven o'clock and still no Jasper.

"Don't worry, he'll be here." Madison smiled. "There's no way Jasper is going to miss this after all he had to go through to get you here."

"I'm not worried. I was just seeing how much time we had left." She brushed it off instead of admitting that her stomach was in knots.

"Yeah, sure." Maddy reached for Jackie's wrist and touched her silver bracelet. "Is this new? It's beautiful."

"Yes." Heat flooded her cheeks. "Jasper's been sending gifts every day. This one arrived this morning."

"It's a Brighton. I love their stuff." Madison let

go so she could greet another newcomer but quickly turned her attention back to the woman at her side. "So what else has he sent?"

"Well, it started with flowers and chocolates."

"I remember those. You were so sure that they were for someone else."

"Then it became other things, such as gift cards, but then the jewelry started to arrive. I got the matching earrings." Lifting her hair, Jackie displayed the Swarovski crystals that glittered on her earlobes. "I probably shouldn't have accepted them, but..."

"But what? If he didn't want you to have them, he wouldn't have given them to you," Madison reassured. "Never look a gift horse in the mouth, as they say."

"I guess so. I'm just not used to the attention." It was the truth. No one had ever pursued her before, and she wasn't sure how to handle the whole situation.

"Just relax and enjoy it." This time it was Madison who checked her watch. "It's time. Let's get everyone seated."

After circling the room, Jackie took a seat at her table. Alone. This didn't make sense. He'd pursued her for over a week yet didn't bother to show up for their date. Was this some kind of sick joke? Not to mention, everyone in the room knew he'd received the biggest bid of anyone. Whenever she risked a look to the front door, it was hard not to notice the looks of sympathy thrown her way.

A waiter showed up at her table and placed their salads on the table, one in front of her and one where Jasper was supposed to be. Tears threatened to fall, but she held them off. A man who didn't show up for an important event didn't deserve to be cried over.

Picking up her fork, she was shocked to see Madison take the seat across from her. "Do you mind if I eat here until we know what happened to Jasp?"

"Thank you. I don't think I can handle any more of the frowns and curious looks people keep throwing my way," Jackie admitted.

"I'm worried something must have happened. I sent a message to Roman, but it went to voicemail."

They ate in silence until Maddy's phone started to vibrate. "It's Roman." A smile always lit up her face whenever he was in the picture. Her face glowed as she answered his call. "I'm good. Everything is going as planned, but where the hell is Jasper?"

The server came to pick up the empty plates and replaced them with surf and turf. The food was delicious, but Jackie had lost her appetite.

"No. He's not here." Madison shook her head.

She leaned across the table and whispered, "He's having the tech guy track his phone."

Tech guys? It was still hard to get a handle on everything that went on in Madison's life. Bodyguards, a tech team, and who knew what else?

"What? Are you serious? Yes, I will let her know." The pained expression on her face had Jackie holding her breath. What the hell had happened? "Yes, I'd love for you to come over. I have a feeling Jackie will want to go check on him."

She paused. "Yes, I love you too." Maddy put the phone away and looked her in the eye. "They tracked his phone, and he's at the hospital."

"What?" The piece of lobster in her mouth almost lodged in her throat. "Was he in an accident?"

"He's not listed as a patient, but he's in the emergency room." Her phone buzzed again. "Wait. It's a text from Jasper. It says, 'I don't have Jackie's number. Please tell her how sorry I am. Something came up. I will make it up to her.' Damn right he will."

"What kind of emergency?" Jackie risked a peek around the room again. Everyone seemed to be enjoying themselves and had forgotten about her empty table, now that Madison had joined her.

"I have no idea, and Roman said it wasn't family business, or he'd know about it."

Jackie let the "family business" comment fly. They didn't seem to be concerned at all about discussing things around her and were all but welcoming her to the "family." It was unsettling, to say the least. She'd been complaining not too long ago about feeling bored, but there was a big difference between being bored and being stupid. She'd eagerly accepted putting a foot into this world, but it was important to keep the other one on the safe side.

"What do you want to do?" Madison sipped her wine.

"Do? I'm working. I can't just leave." She shrugged. "Besides, he didn't say anything about me checking on him."

"That's true, but I know these guys. They never want to be seen as weak. You'll hear from him soon, and he did say he would make it up to you."

It still burned her chops that he hadn't shown up, and she still didn't know why.

"Are you finished here?" So lost in her thoughts, Jackie jumped when the server asked to clear her plate.

"Ah, yes. Thank you." She dabbed at her mouth with the cloth napkin before returning it to her lap.

A few minutes later, he returned with dessert. Normally, she'd be drooling at the sight of chocolate cake and vanilla gelato, but the excitement of the evening had dimmed.

While their guests finished, Madison took to the microphone. She thanked everyone for coming and for their generous donations.

Jackie bit her lip before finishing off her wine. Everyone seemed to be having a wonderful time, everyone but her. Before, she was hurt and disappointed, but now it had changed to anger. How dare he stand her up with no explanation? Sure, he was supposedly in the emergency room, but what did that mean? Had he been drinking with friends and someone fell off a bar stool? Standing up, she brushed some imaginary crumbs from the skirt of her dress. The phrase "all dressed up and nowhere to go" kept ringing through her brain.

"Jackie?" Madison rushed up. "I got things under control, if you wanted to go."

"What?" Obviously, her boss could tell her head was no longer in the game. "Are you sure?"

"Yes. Everyone's just going to mingle while the

workers clean up." When Jackie hesitated, Madison kept talking. "Look, I feel really bad about the ways things ended up. I wanted this to be a fun night for you." She shoved a box and a bottle into her hands. "It's more cake and wine. Go home, relax, and I'll see you Monday."

"Thanks." Jackie raised the bottle up. "I will."

Weaving her way through the crowd that seemed to want to stay and mingle, she finally made it outside. The evening air had cooled, but she was heating up. How dare he lead her on all week, only to drop her like a piece of day-old bread? Jackie unlocked her car and tossed the wine and cake onto the passenger seat.

If he thought he could get away with leaving her high and dry with no explanation, the guy was in for a surprise. Jackie put the car in gear and headed to Genoa's only hospital.

Chapter Eleven

Jackie

Dammit, she'd forgotten her flats at Firenza. The aching in her calves just added to her aggravation as she stomped across the granite floor of the hospital. Now that she was here, it didn't seem like such a wise notion anymore. The man was here for a reason, and she had nothing to do with it, nothing to do with him. There was no good reason to cause a scene in a place like this, even though his no-show hurt like a bitch.

Wringing her hands, she started to turn around. This was a bad idea, and she needed to leave before anyone saw her. It was probably the talk of the town already that she'd been stood up at the dinner tonight. But what if he had been hurt? He was at a hospital.

Ugh!

That man had her upside down and inside out. Still, it was probably best to just leave quietly.

"Jackie?" Crap. It was Jasper. So much for

leaving quietly. "Jackie."

"Yeah." She turned and immediately regretted her anger toward him. There were shadows under his eyes, and even his perfect hair looked off kilter.

"I can't believe you're here." Before she knew it, he'd pulled her into an embrace. "You have no idea how much it means to me that you're here."

"Really? Why are you here? What happened?" Jasper pulled back, took her hand, and led her to a nearby couch.

"My grandfather took a bad fall." He motioned for her to take a seat and sat down beside her.

"Your grandfather?" That was the last thing she expected to hear. She had to stop thinking the worst of this man when he'd done nothing to warrant it except for being a ladies' man. In a way, it was how she was able to keep him at arm's length, when all she really wanted to do was get closer.

"Yes. When I got the call, I raced over here, and I've been waiting ever since." He ran his fingers through his thick, shiny hair, ruffling it more, and the effect made him sexier yet. "I can't believe I never got your number. That's why I had to contact Maddy. It was a jerk thing to do, but I was worried sick."

"It's all right." It was the first time she could recall him being truly vulnerable, and it made him even more appealing. "Have you heard anything yet?"

"No, just that he hit his head on the way down and that they're doing some tests." Jasper rested his elbows on his knees.

It was all she could think of to say. "What's his

name?"

"Frankie. He raised me after my mother died." His voice broke. "He's the only blood relative I have left."

Oh dear, here he'd been sick to death with worry and she'd thought the worst. Jackie took his hand in hers, and his dark eyes met hers. "Tell me about him. About your family."

"You're a reporter, so I know you have a good idea who the Caponellis are."

"I used to be a reporter," she corrected, "and I'm talking about your family, not theirs."

"Once a reporter, always a reporter. That means you're curious, and you don't do anything without knowing what you are getting into."

They both watched a nurse go into the ER before speaking again.

"That may be true, but in this case, I really don't know what I'm doing." She took a deep breath. "I took the job at the winery for a change of pace, but I'm really not sure what I'm doing with my life, and I haven't for a long time."

"You know you work for a mob boss's wife, right?" Jasper leaned back and rested his hands in his lap.

"As much as I try to deny it, I know. I figured the winery was safe, though."

"Wait here." Jasper got up and walked down the hall. He returned a few minutes later with a cup of coffee in each hand. "I know it's not from the Java Shop, but it's warm."

"Thank you." The heated drink hit the spot. He'd added creamer and sugar to hers, just the way she liked it.

"You asked me about my family. Well, this is between you and me. It's off the record, as they say." She nodded. Off the record, meaning it stayed between the two of them and no one else.

"My father grew up in the mob, as did his father," Jasper nodded toward the ER, "and his father before him."

"So it's in the blood. Heritage so to speak." This was the last thing she wanted to hear, but Jackie had known in her heart all along that it was true.

"Yes. Born in blood, die in blood, as the saying goes." He took a sip of his coffee and set it on the table. "My dad died when I was pretty young. Shot to death in a turf war." She reached for his hand, but his engulfed hers first. It was calloused and rough but warm and comforting. Just the thought of that hand trailing along her skin and up her thigh had her shifting in her seat. Now was not the time and place to think along those lines.

"I'm so sorry." It must have been tough losing a parent so young. She knew firsthand how it felt when one was older, and it had changed her life forever.

"Me too. I didn't really know him that well, but I could tell my mother loved him very much, so he must've been good to her." He squeezed her hand. "She said I look a lot like him."

"What happened to her?" Jackie's heart broke asking the question, but the urge to know more about him got the best of her. "You said your grandfather was the only relative left."

"*I* happened to her." Jasper let go of her hand,

stood up, and walked over to a window.

"What do you mean?" She followed.

Indecision marred his face, but he finally spoke. "I was a pretty wild kid. My grandfather, of course, kept me in line as much as he could, but my mother spoiled me."

"I'm imagining a younger version of you. The puppy dog eyes. I bet you had the ladies fawning over you, even at that age. How could a mother resist spoiling you?"

He didn't deny it. "I didn't always listen to her when I should've, and she died because of it." Jasper placed his palms on the windowsill.

"What? No." She placed a hand on his back. His body warm but rigid.

"Yes. I was ten, out playing out in the street, kicking a ball around." He shook his head. "She kept yelling at me to come in and that it was too dangerous to be out there. That I could get hit by a car."

"What happened?" Jackie asked softly.

"She came out to get me." The muscles in his jaw twitched. "I can still see her, fists on her hips. I was being a smartass and refused to move." Jackie could feel the tension coming off him in waves. "Out of nowhere, this truck came barreling down the street. My mom yelled at me to move, but I was frozen. She ran out and pushed me out of the way."

"Oh, no." Her eyes closed. One didn't need to hear the rest to know how the story ended. "She didn't make it."

"No, and the bastard in the truck never stopped." He turned and wrapped his arms about her. He

113

needed a hug and he would get one.

"She sounds like an amazing woman, and she obviously loved you very much."

"Yes, she was. No woman can ever replace your mother. I think that's what I've been doing all these years. Looking for a love that's so unconditional that you'd give your life for each other. So far, I haven't been so lucky." Jasper cupped her cheek in his palm. "Maybe you're the one." The flirty Jasper was back, or was it just his way of pushing sad emotions down below the surface?

"Maybe." For the first time since meeting him, she started to believe it. The man had many layers, and the ones she'd seen were winning her over.

"Jasper?" A blonde rushed her way with Dominic following behind. "What happened? We heard you were here." Jasper hugged the woman and did the half shake hands, half man-hug with Dom.

"Grandfather fell. Just waiting to hear." He pulled Jackie closer. "Do you know my girlfriend, Jackie?"

Both Stephanie and Dom's eyes widened.

"We're...I'm not—" she tried to start before he interrupted.

"Well, she isn't yet, but I keep trying." He grinned and winked her way. The gesture caused her belly to heat and her heart to melt. This was bad, but it felt too good to argue.

"We met last fall at the book signing." Jackie held out her hand. "I worked for the paper then, but now I work with Madison at the winery."

"Oh, yes, I'm sorry we never did have that

interview." Stephanie wrapped her arm around Dominic's waist.

"Well, I'm no longer with the paper, but I'd still like to hear more about the story. If you ever want to do lunch, just let me know."

"I'd like that." Stephanie's head turned to Jasper's, then back to her. "Any friend of Jasper's is a friend of ours."

"Jasper Lencioni?" a doctor called out.

"Here." He grabbed Jackie's hand, and they rushed over to the man.

"Mr. Lencioni said you were his grandson." The man's nametag said, "Doctor Taylor."

"Yes, how's he doing?" Jasper tightened the grip on her hand.

"He's awake. Your grandfather has a mild concussion, and we're keeping him overnight for observation. He's asking to see you now."

"So he'll be okay?"

"In time, yes. He's had a bad fall and needs to take things easy for a while, but I expect a full recovery."

"That's great." Jasper smiled, and Jackie could almost feel the tension leaving his body. "I'd love to see him."

"Of course. Nurse Schlosser will show you the way." He nodded toward the woman in scrubs beside him.

"Great. Thanks." Jasper turned, and Dom and Stephanie were right behind them.

"I'm sorry, but he needs his rest, which means only a short visit and only family." The man was firm on that.

"Call us later," Dom said, and Stephanie gave Jasper a kiss on the cheek before stepping back.

"Yes, let me know also," Jackie added.

"Don't go." Jasper took both of her hands in his. "Please stay and come say hi. He'd loved that."

"But they said only family and that he needs his rest." It didn't seem right to intrude.

"Please." It was hard to decide on which Jasper was harder to resist, the flirty, confident one, or the vulnerable, caring one. Either way, she was a goner. Jackie nodded, and the smile he gave her clipped even more of her icy resolve away. There was no way he wasn't going to break her heart, but it was too late to fight it now.

They followed the nurse down the hall to his grandfather's room. The head of the bed was raised a little, and he was drinking some water from a straw.

"Grampa, you scared the shit out of me." Jasper took the water bottle from his hand and kissed him on the cheek.

"It'll take more than a fall to keep me down." Despite the head injury, the man seemed tough as nails. His grandfather suddenly noticed her presence, raised an eyebrow, and glanced at his grandson. "And who's this?"

"Jackie, meet my grandfather, Francis 'Frankie' Lencioni. Frankie, this is Jackie."

"It's a pleasure." She held out her hand and took it in his.

"The pleasure's all mine. She'd a looker, Jasp. I always did like redheads." He winked and let go of her hand.

"I can see where Jasper gets his charm," Jackie teased as she sat in the chair next to the bed.

"You're both dressed up." He waved his hands. "Don't tell me that my being stupid took you away from a date."

Her gaze met Jasper's. "Well, we did have something, but if you're doing okay by tomorrow, I plan on making it up to her."

"You think so, huh?" It was a given he would, but it didn't hurt to have him sweat a little. "Maybe that was your only chance, and you blew it," she said.

"Well, you did make a bet and lost."

"What?" Her mouth dropped open.

"Don't you remember? You agreed to go on a second date if I got you to go on the first one."

"But we didn't actually go on a date. You bailed." She smirked and crossed her arms over the chest.

"It was an emergency."

Frankie's head went back and forth between the two as if he were at a tennis match. Jackie worried with the injury, he'd get nauseous.

"Please," Frankie held up a hand, "don't make me feel any worse than I already am for ruining your evening." They both reassured him that he hadn't.

"So are we on for tomorrow night?" Jasper glanced down at her with those intoxicating eyes. "I'll make it worth your while."

"You better." Jackie crossed her legs and swung her foot.

"Believe me. It'll be a night you'll never forget."

He dazzled her with those brown puppy dog eyes again. "I promise."

Chapter Twelve

Jasper

Normally, he'd be all up for a job. Sparring with an opponent kept his skills sharp, kept him on his toes, kept him alive. Today, he just wasn't feeling it. Jasper could feel the bruise rise around his eye. It hurt like a bitch, and it was the last thing he needed when he had a date tonight. Exhaustion had him sluggish. After seeing Jackie home and stopping at his place for a change of clothes, he returned to sleep in a chair by his grandfather's hospital bed, just in case he needed anything. Frankie was doing fine, but still, he couldn't help but worry.

Arlo woke him early with a call and asked to meet him outside the hospital. Roman had been asked to do a favor for the local MC club, the Tribe of Mayhem, which meant they were the ones to get their hands dirty. A rival gang member had broken into their warehouse and stolen a bunch of guns. They'd located the guy, Ray, and it was now up to Arlo and Jasper to get the guns back.

Some jobs where supposed to be easy, but those seldom were. A dog ruined their surprise attack at the man's house. That's where a fist to the face had almost fractured Jasper's eye socket. For a skinny fucker, Ray was quick on his feet but not fast enough to get away from the two of them. Now he was tied to a folding chair in the middle of a shed.

Jasper held his palm to his cheek, hoping the coolness of his hand would help with the swelling. Unfortunately, it was hotter than hell, even in the morning, especially in the closed garage, where they'd brought the man to interrogate and work him over. Jasper hadn't been here since Dominic had to fight to keep Stephanie, and now, they were getting married. How quickly things had changed.

Roman was on his way, and with a glance out the door, Jasper could see his boss's SUV blowing up dust along the way. Oscar was with him today, and they were being escorted by several of the Tribe crew.

"How can one place be so damn cold one part of the year and hotter than hell the rest?" Arlo wiped his forehead with the back of his hand. "Kind of like a certain woman I know," he added under his breath.

Jasper chuckled as he walked to Roman's car. Arlo had it bad for Layla. Jasper didn't really know her that well, but she was Madison's half sister and the ultimate mafia princess daughter to a rival family in Chicago. It would take a miracle for those two to get together, but stranger things had happened. Such as the fight to the death that Dominic had won to break the marriage contract

Stephanie had been bound to with a Russian mafia family. Dating in the mob was not for the faint of heart.

Roman stepped into the garage and tucked his sunglasses into his suitcoat pocket. It could be 200 degrees out and the guy would still be decked out in an Armani suit and tie. The man was his idol.

"Has he said anything?" His boss came to stand beside him.

"We haven't asked yet. Figured we'd wait and see what you wanted us to do." Jasper followed Roman and the club members over to Ray.

The club's president, Forge, stood in front of Ray. His face was bright red, but it was most likely not from the heat. They'd have handled this themselves, but because it involved the guns bought from the Caponellis, they wanted Roman's crew to be there also.

"Where are they?" Forge narrowed his eyes.

"Where's what?" Ray struggled in the chair.

"We have video tape of you breaking into our building and stealing our guns."

This time, Ray looked away. His tough attitude was slipping now that reinforcements had arrived.

"Where are they?" Forge shook the guy.

"I don't know shit," he spat.

Forge stepped aside, and Roman motioned Jasper to get to work. Walking over to a work table, he surveyed what was available. Putting on some rubber gloves, he picked up a pair of tools. Some preferred shoving needles under people's fingernails and stuff like that, but he was old-school. If it worked, why change?

121

It was hard to hold back the yawn from lack of sleep as he strolled over to the man in the chair. Sometimes delaying the torture was enough to get the person to spill. He wanted this over quickly so he could take a nap. He had pliers in one hand and a hammer in the other.

"What the hell are you going to do with that?" Ray squeaked and tried to skid his chair back with his feet, but he wasn't going anywhere.

"The hammer is to keep your mouth open." Jasper slammed the head of the hammer on Ray's hand. When Ray yelled, he shoved the wood part into the guy's mouth. "While I pull your teeth out with the pliers. Ready?" Jasper flashed him a smile, while Arlo held the man's head in place. Moving the hammer to one side, Jasper started with the front teeth. With only one root, they come out easily. Four down and out, he pulled the tool out of Ray's mouth.

"You ready to answer the questions now?" Jasper held his hands dripping with blood over the plastic-covered floor. He didn't want to risk get anything on his clothes while he deposited the teeth in a nearby bucket.

"I don't know. I don't know." Ray frothed at the mouth.

"But you do admit to taking them." Roman stepped closer, but not close enough to dirty his Dolce & Gabbana shoes.

"Yeah, hell. Whatever, I took them. I was just hoping to find something to steal and make some money." Jasper moved to the side as the guy spit blood with every "S" he spoke. "When I saw the guns, I knew I could sell them."

"You sold them?" Forge growled. "To who?"

"I can't tell you. If I do, they'll kill me." Ray was covered in sweat and smelled like hell.

"What do you think we'll do to you if you don't tell us?" Roman's voice echoed in the cavernous building.

"I can't." Ray shook his head, and Jasper shoved the hammer into his mouth again. This time, he took two molars. The guy would have to chew with the one side of his mouth from now on. Actually, the man wouldn't be eating again. Ever. It was a given that the guy wouldn't be leaving the place alive.

When he removed the hammer this time, Jasper dropped it to the floor. "Look, we can do this all day. Once your teeth are all gone, we'll find something else to remove."

Ray's breathing elevated, and his chin was on his chest. Jasper lifted it up and stared into his glazed over eyes. "Who. Has. The. Guns?"

Ray mumbled something. "Speak up." Jasper gave him a slap on the face. This time, Forge stepped closer, and they both heard what he said.

"Those bastards," Forge cursed. Ray had sold them to a man with a Russian accent named Dimitri. "Now, we have the fucking Russian mob here?" He directed the comment toward Roman, who, in turn, filled them in on the woman who had been found along the side of the road. "That's the last thing I wanted to hear. I don't mess with the bratva. That's your deal. But if they have our guns, I want them back. Let me know what else you find out." Forge shook hands with Roman and nodded to Jasper and

Arlo. "Okay, men. Let's go." The gang left the building, and their bikes soon roared to life outside.

"What do we do with this guy?" Arlo had been quiet for most of the time but now seemed eager to get the hell out of there.

"Kill him, and call Dom." Roman put his sunglasses back on and walked out the door.

Nothing felt better than a hot shower after a long night and day. It was dirty work dealing with a dead body, and it pissed him off to no end that the fucker had given him a black eye. Jasper had taken a quick nap after getting home, so he felt refreshed for the first time in twenty-four hours.

He dressed with care. Blue shirt, navy striped suspenders, and navy dress pants. His tie was accented with white and blue. Everything was all set, and before the night was over, Jackie wouldn't know what hit her. There was no end to the surprises he'd lined up. The first being a new dress. With the help of Madison, she picked out a matching blue dress for her. Maddy made sure it had arrived at Jackie's door this morning.

Most would think he was trying to buy the woman, but that wasn't the truth. He'd never paid for anything for a woman before. Sure, he'd paid for meals, but this was different. The gifts had meaning behind them. They were meant to show he'd take care of her, cherish her, and always be there to give her anything she needed. Life was different in the mob. There were traditions to uphold, and providing for loved ones was a biggie. Did he love Jackie? It was too early for that, but given time, he knew they'd be perfect together.

He'd gone out with enough women to know what he did and didn't like. Jackie had spunk, smarts, and a sense of humor. She was the whole package and one who would keep him interested for a lifetime.

She was the good to his evil, the dawn to his night. The cleanness that he needed in his life to wipe away the mud. It didn't hurt that he thought she was sexy as hell and the most beautiful woman he'd ever laid eyes on.

A glance at his watch and Jasper grabbed his suitcoat and walked out the door.

Jackie

Her fingers shook as she tried to fasten the new bracelet around her wrist. It was gorgeous and another piece of Brighton jewelry that had arrived today, courtesy of her date for the evening. There would come a day when those gifts stopped coming. All good things came to an end, but for now, she was going to enjoy them while they lasted.

The bracelet flew out of her hand when the doorbell rang. Dang it. He was here. Jackie felt like a teenager as she picked the jewelry up off the floor and hurried barefooted to the door. Drool almost fell from her mouth when she saw how handsome he looked in his blue outfit that matched hers. His hair was flawless, as always, and his eyes had that flirty twinkle to them. Except one that was swollen and bruised.

"What happened to your eye?" She waved him inside and shut the door.

"It's nothing." He gave her the once-over with

his eyes and let out a wolf whistle. "You look amazing."

"Do you like it?" She twirled around in her fitted off-the-shoulder dress. "Madison picked it out. Did you know she gave up being a dress designer to stay here and marry Roman?"

"Yup. True story and true love." He motioned to the bracelet in her hand. "Do you need help with that?"

"Yes, please. I was just putting it on when the bell rang." He quickly secured the clasp and took her hand in his. The man could probably feel how rapidly her heart beat. It was hard to be cool around Jasper. He oozed confidence and sex appeal like no other. "I love it, but you really need to stop getting me things. I'm already spoiled."

"I like spoiling you. It makes me happy to pick out things for you."

"I don't know what you like." Jackie braced a hand on the back of the couch to slip on her shoes.

"I like you." He winked.

Could this man get any better? He'd rival any book boyfriend she'd ever read about. Reaching for the wrap she'd chosen to keep the chill away, Jasper took it from her hands and draped it over her shoulder.

"We'd better get going. We don't want to miss the boat."

"Boat?" The chance to get out on the lake was something she'd wanted to do ever since arriving in Genoa.

"Yes, a dinner cruise." Jasper held his elbow out, and she tucked her hand into the crease. Whether it was intended or not, this felt like the start of what could end up being the most romantic evening of her life. After walking out of her building, Jasper opened the door to his SUV, and they drove the short distance to the dock.

The warm sun caressed her shoulders as they walked through the park to the Riviera Pavilion. The Pavilion had been built back in the 1930s and featured a ballroom upstairs. There must have been a party or wedding reception going on, as people in tuxes and long dresses climbed up and down the stairs to the upper level. The floor level featured little gift and food shops. Jasper and Jackie strolled the area and went outside by the docks. All kinds of different boats in the local cruise fleet could be seen. They had eight in total of all sizes from a forty-one-foot cruiser to vintage double-decker steam boats.

A group of people headed toward the Grand Belle for the sunset cruise, and Jackie followed suit.

"Where're you going?" Jasper stood on the dock with his hand in his pocket.

"Ah, I thought we were going on the dinner cruise." He must have bought tickets, as it was by reservations only, and they didn't want to hold up the ship.

"We are, but you can't go without this." The necklace he pulled out of his pocket sparkled in the early evening sun. Even from a distance, the silver chain and crystals sparkled.

"Jasper. No. Like I said, you're spoiling me." And setting too high of a standard for any other man she might date. It wasn't just the gifts, but the fact that he wanted her to feel special and had taken the time to pick everything out for her.

"You don't want?" he teased and put it back in his pocket.

"Well, I didn't say that." It was hard to resist.

Jasper made her turn around as he placed the necklace around her neck. "I liked the setting when I first saw it. Dianna, the saleslady, told me it was from the infinity collection." It matched several of the other pieces he'd given her. Jasper stepped in front of her. "In the family, we choose a woman for life. For infinity."

"It's stunning. I love it." The metal was cool against her skin, but her heart was aflame. She was giddy and almost jumped up and down. That was, until she noticed their boat starting to leave the dock. "Jasper, it's leaving. We're missing the cruise."

"No, we're not." He reached for her arm as she started to wave for them to stop.

"What do you mean? I thought we were going on a boat."

"We are, but we're not taking that one," he corrected.

"But that's the only one that hosts the dinner cruises." Her stomach groaned. "We can go somewhere else, but I hate the fact that you'll be out of the money for the tickets."

"Don't worry. I didn't pay for that boat." Jasper took her hand in his and started down the dock. "I paid for this one." They stopped in front of an enormous vintage vessel. One that was waiting just for them.

Jackie may not have left land yet, but she'd already been swept away.

Chapter Thirteen

Jackie

Ahead was something out of a fairytale. Jasper had rented a private yacht—one of the vintage boats built back in the late 1880s. A steward stood on the deck in front holding a tray with two glasses of champagne.

"Jasper." That's all she could manage to say as he guided her onto the boat with a hand to her lower back, and they both took a glass. The boat was big enough to fit fifty or more people, but it was all for them. One table sat in the middle toward the front deck. The shiny gold silverware reflected the light from the candles atop the crisp white tablecloth. "This is too much."

"Nothing's too much for you." Jasper took her hand and led her to the front of the ship as the crew pushed off from the dock and started their cruise. "You see those flowers on the table?"

"Purple roses. Yes. They were on the table the other night."

"The night I missed our date. I'm really sorry about that."

"You're forgiven. You had a good excuse." She turned toward the flowers again. "I've never seen such beautiful flowers before."

"Do you know what they stand for?" Maddy had told her, but she wanted to hear what he had to say.

"Love at first sight." Jasper touched the edge of his glass to hers and took a drink. "When I saw you last fall, I thought you were the most intriguing and beautiful woman I'd ever met, and I know a lot of smart and good-looking chicks. Madison, Valentina, Stephanie."

It was hard not to giggle, but she did. It was overwhelming. "Well, thank you. You're not so bad yourself, but I hardly think it was love at first sight, since I turned you down and we hadn't seen each other since."

"That's true, but all winter long, things have been off for me. It's like there's been something missing in my life. Then you came along again, and I knew what it was."

"Me?" It was too good to believe, but he nodded yes. "Why me?"

"Who knows?" He chuckled and glanced toward the water as a wooden-hulled boat passed by. "Do we ever really know what it is about a person that makes us love them or hate them? It's just a feeling. One that starts as friendship and grows into a relationship. Something that goes on endlessly, just like the swirls of the jewelry I gave you."

"I never pegged you as such a romantic, but it just seems too early to be talking about love and

131

forever when we haven't known each other that long." It may be too early, but he was again chipping away at her guarded heart with a jackhammer.

"Not for me. In this family, relationships are for a lifetime. That's why I'm being so up front with you. Dating outside the mob is frowned upon. We value loyalty and trust over everything. Wives and girlfriends hear things and see things that they shouldn't; we have to know that they're in it for the long haul. That's why I did all of this." Jasper touched the necklace around her neck and gestured toward the table that held the bouquet. "It's symbolism, but it's true. I wanted you to know ahead of time what you were getting into. I want to date you, be with you, make love with you, but this is a lifestyle and a lifetime. I want you to understand that this is real for me, and I'm not just messing around."

"Wow, and this is only our second date." The whole thing was overwhelming. "Well, first actually, since we didn't make the real first date."

"I believe in being honest and forthright." A dazzling smile lit up his face. "You don't have to decide anything right now, but I just wanted you to know where I stand."

All she could do was nod. What did a person say to that?

"I know it's a lot to take in, but I wanted you to know what you were getting into." He took her hand and kissed the inside of her palm. Jasper did something to her that no man ever had before. He made her feel special, desired, and wanted.

"Madison and Stephanie? Were they warned before also?" It all made her head spin. Dating was hard enough without thinking about the added complications of getting involved with the Caponelli family, but nothing bad had happened yet. Actually, things were great. She had a job she loved and made amazing new friends.

"Yes, and Maddy fought it like crazy, from what I hear. She wanted nothing to do with Roman, but he changed her mind."

"Well, thank you for telling me." It was true. Getting involved with a made man was something she'd never even considered doing, but as she slowly got to know the people she worked with, they were growing on her and had become her friends. This time, he kissed the top of her head. Funny how she'd never let a guy get this close in public, yet he could probably undress her on the deck of this ship and kiss every square inch without her telling him to stop.

"Let's sit down and eat." He finished his drink just as the steward came to retrieve their empty glasses.

The meal was wonderful. All her favorites: wedged salad with fresh Roquefort, followed by a main course of filet mignon and loaded baked potatoes. The cool lake air caused her to scoot her chair closer to the man by her side, and he draped his jacket over her bare shoulders. The wrap she brought was clearly for looks and not warmth. The jacket smelled like him, a light outdoorsy cologne and all man. She pulled it tighter and inhaled.

Her resolve was waning. A girl would have

133

nothing to complain about with this man. Well, except for the criminal activities. She had no clue of what he really did do, and frankly, right now, it was the last thing on her mind.

"I can't believe the amazing homes along this lake." The stewards brought coffee and dessert as Jasper placed his hand on her knee. It was comforting and intoxicating all at once.

"See that one over there?" He pointed toward a large home with a Mediterranean look to it.

"Yes."

"That's Roman and Madison's house. The one next to it belongs to Ryan and Valentina. Her father gave it to them for a wedding present."

"Wow. Nice gift." Never would she have guessed at the wealth of the people she worked for. They all treated her like family, and they were so down to earth. "Does everyone in the family live on the lake?" She used air quotes for "family."

"No, Dominic and Stephanie live out in the country in a cabin. It's on a lake but a smaller one. I live in an old restored home downtown, as does Arlo when he's in town, only he has a condo. He's been helping Madison's family out with some things and goes back and forth. Some of the married guys have homes in town or just outside."

"It's a nice town. I wasn't sure if I'd like it here at first, after living in bigger cities all my life, but it's growing on me." But could she stay when everything was said and done?

"It's a great place to raise a family."

"Don't tell me you're already planning how many kids we'll have." She'd not felt this happy in years.

"I love how you said 'we,' but no, just saying." He winked and picked up his fork. A large piece of chocolate cake with vanilla ice cream and strawberries for dessert completed their delicious meal.

The first bite resulted in a moan of satisfaction. "This is wicked good."

"Someday, you'll be moaning against me and saying the same thing." Jasper pierced a berry with his fork and held it up for her to take a bite.

"You're better than chocolate cake? You must be very impressive in bed." The guy was too much, but she wouldn't mind finding out if he could back up that statement.

"So I've been told." His chest puffed out, but she just rolled her eyes. "But if you agree to be with me, it'll only be you, forever. For infinity."

There it was again. That pact to be committed. It was like being hot and cold at the same time. Her head spun from sensory overload. Romantic setting, delicious food, gorgeous man, and welcome to the mafia. Forever.

"I just need a little more time to process everything."

"That's understandable." Jasper smiled. "You have a week to decide."

"What?" She almost choked on the cake. "Are you serious?"

"Yes. I don't want you to overthink things. You either know or you don't. I want you, Jackie, but if you don't see a future between us, I don't want to wait around forever for something that's never going to happen."

"I can understand that. Life is precious." His grandfather's fall could have been so much worst. If he'd hit his head and cracked his skull, they could be planning a funeral now.

"It is, and if anything were to ever happen to me, you'd be surrounded by people that will always take care of you. Look after you," he added.

The wonderful cake suddenly tasted dry. "Do you think something will happen to you?"

"You never know. It's a dangerous life, but so is driving home at night."

Her thoughts turned to her parents—a simple night out that suddenly ended everything. The spring evening had turned colder, and the crew had pulled down the plastic sides to block the wind. They turned around back near the end of the main course, and the boat now neared the dock. It would be hard to leave such a magical evening, but all great things must come to an end.

Jasper left a hefty tip for the crew, and with purple flowers in hand, they left the boat.

"Let's walk back. It's such a nice night, and I like having you by my side."

"Sounds good." Taking her hand, he led her down the dock.

The other cruise boat had just gotten back also, so couples were strolling around laughing and having a good time.

"Jasper," Jackie pulled him to a stop, "I have to say, that has to be the best date and nicest thing that anyone has ever done for me."

"Making you happy makes me happy." He drew

her close and wrapped his arm around her shoulders, which were still covered with his jacket.

"How is your grandfather doing?" In all the excitement, she'd forgotten to ask.

"Much better. He's getting out tomorrow, and I and a few of the guys will be helping move him into a housing development with easier living, everything on one floor. He'll have his own place and everything, but no steps to fall on."

"Do you need any more help moving boxes?" The guy had a kind heart, and she wouldn't mind spending more time in a relaxed setting.

"No, but I'm sure Grandpa would love to see you, if you want to stop by later." Jasper gave her the address, and she knew where that was. The paper she'd worked for had covered the opening of the complex.

"I might do that." Emphasis on the *might.* Jackie didn't want to commit to anything tonight that she might regret in the morning. Getting closer to these people didn't seem like a good idea if she wasn't planning on staying. Before moving here, Jackie had promised herself that if she didn't find what she was searching for, or life didn't fall in place in that amount of time, she'd move on.

But what if she did stay?

They walked in silence for the last couple blocks, their steps getting even slower as they neared her home. Jasper saw her to the front door and leaned against the wall as she unlocked the door.

"I'd invite you in, but right now, my head is going crazy, and like you said, I need to think before we act."

"And that's exactly what I want you to do." He moved closer and placed her palm over his heart. "I also want you to remember how much you make my heart race. And I want you to remember this." Jasper touched his lips to hers.

What started as a slow, savoring kiss became an intense mind-blowing kiss to end all others. His arms wrapped around her lower back and pulled her closer. So close she could feel his hard length pressing into her belly. It was a good thing he held her tight, as he made her knees weak. The man tasted sweet like ice cream and cake. He then started on her neck, dropping kisses all the way to the top of her shoulder.

When they finally came up for air, her legs wobbled like they were still on the boat.

"Sleep tight, Angel, and dream of me." He kissed her one more time before walking away.

It took every bit of strength to not ask him to stay.

Jackie closed the door behind her and leaned against it as she touched her fingers to her lip. "I am so fucked."

Chapter Fourteen

Jasper

He had it bad. The hard-on he had for Jackie kept him up all night, and erasing the comfort with his hand just wasn't cutting it anymore. He wanted her and only her. The sexual encounters with women in the past now seemed less that satisfying, and there was no urge to go out and search for a nameless hookup. This must have been what maturity finally kicking in felt like.

Jasper shook his head as he pulled in and parked in front of his grandfather's new place. It was a nice complex. There were four units to a building with everyone having their own garage and front yard. It was pretty nice, actually, with a center building in the middle that people could share for private events and get-togethers. His grandfather sat next to him in his vehicle. "What do you think?" The man had always been independent, so moving into a different home would be an adjustment for a while.

"What can I say? It sucks to be old." They both

unbuckled their seat belts. "But I think it will be all right. I met some of the neighbors when I checked it out, and they seemed okay. I didn't want to be in the middle of a bunch of old farts." At that moment, an attractive woman with silver hair stepped outside to water her flowers. Frankie waved at the lady, and she returned the gesture. "Yeah, I don't think it will be too bad at all."

"Checking out the chicks already. You always were the lady's man," Jasper ribbed.

"It runs in the family." Frankie poked him in the side with his elbow.

They'd parked behind Dominic's van. The moving company had brought over most of the heavy stuff on Friday but had to stop when Frankie had fallen at his old place. Arlo and Dom had brought over the rest.

"I hope you cleaned that van before loading everything," Frankie joked as he slowly moved forward to shake each man's hand. Even his grandfather knew about Dom's roll of being the cleaner for the family. Many a dead body had been placed in the back of the vehicle, but no one would ever know it.

"Of course not," he joked. Everyone knew it was spotless, but Dom enjoyed messing with the man anyway.

"Well, let's get this show on the road." Frankie entered the front door of his new place. "I got new neighbors to meet."

A police cruiser stopped next to the van, and Ryan hopped out. "Hey, guys."

Arlo and Dom grabbed some boxes, nodded, and

headed to the house.

"What's up?" Jasper walked to the car as Ryan got something out of the passenger side.

"Valentina sent this over." It was a potted plant. "She'd have come herself, but the little one fussed all night, and they both finally got to sleep."

"Thanks. Frankie's inside, if you want to come in." Jasper motioned toward the house.

"Sorry. Can't stay. The woman who was attacked finally woke up and started to remember things. I need to get caught up on all the latest."

"I hope they find the fucker. Has anyone else been hurt?" God, he hoped not.

"No, but the first thing she remembered was what he was driving." Ryan placed a hand on the side of Dom's vehicle. "A white van."

"Well, we know it isn't this one."

"Yes, we do, but the other guys on the force may not. Make sure Dom doesn't have anything he doesn't want discovered in the back, in case someone decides to pull him over just to check and see." Having a friend on the force was priceless.

"Thanks for letting me know. I'll share the info with the guys. I know Roman is having the tech guys keeping an eye out for the creep." Ryan handed the plant over and said his farewell. Jasper waved and watched him drive away before setting the Hosta outside the front door.

The guys continued to grab the rest of the boxes, and in less than thirty minutes, the van was unpacked, and all Frankie's possessions were inside.

Frankie took a seat on the couch. "I need some

pictures to hang." Everyone glanced at the bare walls.

"I know where you can get a Picasso." Jasper smirked. He'd shared with his grandfather their new venture.

"I don't need any of the fancy stuff, just something to look at."

"I'll see if I can find you a velvet Elvis somewhere," Arlo added.

"What do you think of this side job?" He was referring to the new goods stored at the winery. Frankie was old school and only liked the tried and true businesses.

"I don't know. Some of that shit has tripled in price, but I agree with you. I'd rather be out busting chops and making runs, but I guess we'll see how this goes." Jasper rubbed his chin. He needed a shave.

"Did the club get their guns back?" Frankie kept up to date on all that was going on.

"Not yet, but when we do, I'll be busy collecting the pieces of those fuckers," Dom responded. "No one steals from the Tribe or the family and gets away with it."

A knock sounded on the screen door while they were inside the living room, and Frankie went to answer it.

"Hey, beautiful," Jasper heard his grandfather say.

Arlo piped in, "The new neighbor must have spied the plant and decided to come over and water it." They all laughed, and Jasper's ears perked up when he heard Jackie's voice.

"I'm glad to see you up and about," she gushed over the old man, and he was probably loving every minute of it.

Jasper rose and moseyed toward the two, when what he really wanted to do was run over and gather her in his arms.

"Hey, buster, stop making moves on my girl," he joked before relieving Jackie of the large box in her hand. "What's all this?" The delicious smell of Italian food permeated from the box.

"Madison asked me to pick this up and bring it over. She ordered a bunch of food for the guys and Mr. Lencioni."

"It's Frankie to you, sweetheart." Frankie winked at her before taking a seat at the kitchen table. The man put on a brave front, but he was still a little shaky and weak.

"I told you, old man, stop putting the moves on my girl," Jasper teased as he took the remaining bags that were draped over her arms. She blushed while starting to unpack the paper plates and utensils.

"Everyone can see she only has eyes for you, dumbass." Frankie's comment caused her face to brighten even more.

"Well, like I said, it's nice to see you out of the hospital, and this looks like a great place to live." Jackie opened the box, and it was packed to the top with goodies. More than the five of them could eat, but at least Frankie would have leftovers for a few days.

There was Caesar salad, bread, and two huge containers of spaghetti and ravioli. The other bags held cheesecake, cannoli, and different kinds of meats and cheeses. "Look at all this food they sent. This is amazing."

"Pops, you got anything here to drink?" Jasper opened the refrigerator, but other than a half-gallon of milk and a few beers, there wasn't much there.

"Oh, I almost forgot that's in the trunk. They sent wine, beer, and a new coffee maker too," Jackie volunteered.

"Here, I'll help get that." Jasper ushered her out the door as the smell of food drew Arlo and Dom into the kitchen.

Trailing her down the sidewalk was an exercise in self-control. She wore skin tight blue jeans that showed off her tight ass to perfection. Her hair was up in a sexy bun, and her teal t-shirt made her pale skin look golden. Jackie wore tan sandals, while dark purple nail polish dotted her toes. What pretty toes she had. Yeah, he had it bad for her. Why she was different from the other girls he had met was hard to explain. Maybe it was that she played hard to get and wasn't so easily taken in by his charm. She was smart; there was no doubt about that. Sometimes he could almost see the wheels turning in her mind as if she were trying to figure him out.

"It was really nice of them to send all this stuff. There's probably over a hundred dollars' worth of food, and this is a really nice coffee maker." Opening the trunk, she revealed a couple cases of wine, beer, and the coffee machine.

"This is what I was talking to you about last night. We're a family. Everyone looks out for each other. It's not just about getting stuff. It's that people care."

"So, if I get involved with you, I also gain a mob boss, several hitmen, and a cleaner?" She raised an eyebrow.

"And a free coffee maker," he joshed. "It's a package deal, so to speak." His heart beat faster. Was she considering it? It was easy to see why most guys married women already in their circle. It made things a lot easier, but sometimes, things that were the hardest to get were the most worthwhile. "I'm really glad Madison asked you to come today."

"She didn't." Jackie shut the trunk and turned to face him. Even dressed casually, and with little makeup, she was a beauty. Wait? Maddy didn't ask her to come here?

"She didn't?" he pondered. This morning was getting better and better.

"No. Maddy called and invited me to a brunch today, but when I told her I was thinking about visiting you and your grandfather, she got excited and insisted I bring all this stuff over." The sunlight brought out the different colors of red in her hair, and he gave in to the urge to tuck a stray strand behind her ear. They'd have the cutest kids, but that was too far in the future to think about now.

"Well, I will have to send her a thank you." They started toward the house. It felt right having her here, and it would hurt like hell if she ended up saying no to being his woman. No one liked an ultimatum, but for once in his life, he wasn't fucking around. Literally and figuratively. Life could be short in the mob. His father was proof of that. If anything ever happened to him, he wanted to make sure Jackie had everything she ever needed. It was crazy to think of her as his already, but he knew in his heart it was right.

Soon, everyone was in the living room, going through some old photo albums that Frankie had found.

"Hey, Jasp. Is this you?" Arlo held up a photo of a baby with a lot of dark hair.

"If it's a beautiful baby, it must be," Jasper joked. The others groaned. He was Frankie's only grandchild. He'd been a chubby kid and an awkward teenager, but his grandfather always made him feel special and as if he were the best kid in the world. Maybe he was just trying to help him overcome the grief and guilt he felt, but that would never go away. His love for his grandfather would never dim.

"Can I see?" Jackie reached for the photo, and a smile lit up her face. "So cute."

"There's a whole book of pics of the little devil, if you want to see." Frankie pulled a photo album from a crate and patted a spot next to him on the couch.

"I would." She took a seat and crossed her legs.

"I'm going to get something to eat and head out." Arlo and Dom both exited as fast as possible to the kitchen, while Jasper eased into the recliner.

For the next hour, Frankie went through the pages of Jasper's young life. It touched his heart to learn that there was not just one album but three. What would he have done without this man? What would he have become without this man? Yes, he lived a violent life, but that was a part of their heritage. The legacy of their line. Frankie was one of the lucky ones who had lived to tell the story, but would he?

Arlo and Dom left as soon as they finished lunch. It was getting late, and Jackie was still here, visiting with his grandfather. He yawned, and it was clear the move had worn the elderly man down.

"Is there anything else you need us to help you with?" Clearly, Jackie had noticed it also, as she began picking up dishes and throwing them in the trash.

"You don't need to do that." His grandfather took a plate from her hand and put it in himself. "Both of you, shoo. Go have some fun. You've spent enough time with this old fart."

"Are you sure?" Jasper was tired also.

"Yes, now go." He thanked Jackie again and gave her a quick hug and a kiss on the cheek. "Both of you," Frankie added, while embracing Jasper before ushering them out the door.

Jackie was quiet as Jasper walked with her to her car.

"Thanks for being here today." He stopped in front of her.

"It was nice. I had fun."

"I hate to ask this, but I have a favor to ask." A favor? When had he ever asked this of a girl?

"Sure. What is it?" She bounced from one foot to the other. A chill had settled in the air. From the breeze and humidity in the air, it felt like rain.

"Come to my place tonight."

She can't say no if you don't ask.

"Please."

147

Chapter Fifteen

Jackie

Her headlights flicked off as she parked behind his vehicle in the driveway. Never did she expect to be spending time here tonight. It was still early, so that was why she'd agreed, or at least, that's what Jackie told herself. He was too tempting, and she was already falling hard and fast. This was the last thing she needed to be doing, but maybe there would be some clue he'd let loose. A snippet into what the Caponellis were doing. Were they really going legit, as Madison wanted them to be?

A flash of lightning flickered in the distance. A storm was coming. The first one of the season was always exciting and fresh, but it just elevated the nervousness that had already surfaced. There was nothing to fear, he'd promised her after the invitation.

That's what every spider tells the fly he invites over to hang in their web.

It was her weakness for the man that worried her, not that she was in danger.

Jasper promised to never make her do anything she wasn't ready for or didn't wish to do, and so far, he'd kept his word. The problem was, with each day, there were more and more things she was ready and wishing to do—with him and only him.

Getting out of her car, she looped her purse over her shoulder and walked to where he stood by his car.

"Looks like rain." Just then, large drops started to land on the concrete by their feet. "We made it just in time. Come on in." He unlocked the door and ushered her inside.

Jasper's place was nice. Very nice. It was a charming, century-old home that had been refurbished with all the modern upgrades yet kept its old-world character. It was in a great location close to downtown and all the great shops and restaurants. A so-called hipster spot, but he didn't strike her as such.

"So why did you want me to come over?" Jackie entered the front door and surveyed his living space. For some reason, the expectation was that it would be either messy or impeccably neat. It was neither. The place was tidy but lived in.

"You look surprised." Jasper motioned for her to sit on the couch.

"About you asking me here or about my opinion of your place?" It felt wonderful to sink into the plush leather sofa as she set her purse on the end table.

"Both. What do you want to drink?" He opened the door of the stainless-steel refrigerator. It was hard not to look as he bent to grab a beer. The man had an ass that was to die for. "I have beer, wine, some pop, wine coolers, water, OJ, and milk."

"You don't seem like a wine cooler and milk kind of guy." She crossed her legs.

"You know what they say. It does a body good." He rubbed his hand over his chest in mock adoration and flashed her the breathtaking smile. "I bought the wine coolers in case you ever stopped by."

His confession kicked her in the gut. The man was truly sweet, and she would not be able to put up much resistance any longer. "I'll take one of those then."

Grabbing a bottle from the fridge, he opened it and handed her a bottle of raspberry lemonade. She took a sip. "My favorite. How did you know?"

"You look like a," he reached over to read the label on the bottle, "raspberry lemonade kind of girl," he joked. "Back to my question. Why did you finally agree to come over, and what do you think of the place?"

"What can I say? You're growing on me." It was true. As much as she fought it, she was tumbling head over heels for the guy, and there was no way that would end well for either one of them. They were from two different worlds. "And I like the place. I have to say, I truly didn't know what to expect."

"Here," he offered his hand to help her up, "let me give you a tour."

She reached for it and stood. "I bet you say this to all the girls you bring here. Are you going to show me the bedroom first?" With her hand still in his, it would be so easy to take a step and pull him closer. Jasper was becoming her caramel latte, something she wanted to taste every day but that probably wasn't healthy for her.

"You're the first woman I've ever brought here, and no, you don't get to see the bedroom unless you're spending the night." He lifted an eyebrow in the flirty way that caused her belly to warm. "Are you?"

"Ah, no, but seriously. You've never brought a girl home?" He led her to the kitchen.

"Nope. For right now, this is my home. I would never bring a casual hookup here." Jasper dropped her hand, only to brush his thumb across her cheek. "You're not casual, Angel. You're special."

If it were possible for her heart to grow, it increased in size. Her lip quivered and her eyes watered. She'd not gotten much sleep last night, and fatigue was making her emotional. At least, she wanted to blame it on that. It was the man in front of her who had her hormones raging.

"Hey, what's wrong?" His hand cupped her cheek, and she leaned into it.

"Nothing. It's just that," she gazed up into his beautiful eyes, "no one's ever called me special except for my parents."

"Then you've been hanging out with the wrong people." His thumb caressed her lip before dropping to the side of her throat. There was no way he wouldn't be able to feel the throbbing of her heartbeat there. Jasper dropped a kiss to her lips as her eyes fluttered shut. It was tender, sweet, and way too short. Again, not what she expected from this man.

"Let me show you around. I honestly didn't bring you here to put the moves on." Now it was her turn to lift an eyebrow in question. "I'm serious. Since you're going to be my woman, I thought we should get to know each other better."

Jackie couldn't hold in the laugh. "You are crazy. Why do you think I'll be your woman?"

"Like you just said, I'm growing on you." This time, his hand moved to her waist, and she didn't even think of saying no. "In case you didn't know, this is the kitchen."

"Really? I'd never guess." She'd only taken a sip of the alcohol, so it must have been that this guy that was making her giddy. "Do you cook?"

"I'm no chef, but I'll never starve."

"That's nice to know."

He guided her through the few rooms downstairs before leading her back to the living room. The place had an open floor plan, and pretty much everything was in sight. It was also clean and tidy. For some reason, she'd been half expecting knives, guns, and bodies to be littering the area. "There's a patio off the bedroom upstairs. It's a nice place to sit outside in the morning and look at the lake."

"Just like my place."

"Well, almost. Yours is much closer. Have a seat."

She returned to the couch, and he sat beside her. Not as near as she'd have liked, but he was being a gentleman and not trying to push. At least physically, anyway. Calling her his woman wasn't very subtle.

Jasper picked up the remote. "Anything special you want to watch?"

"We should have gone to my place. I DVR'd the fights last night. I was going to watch them this evening."

"You watch MMA. Okay, now I'm in love with you." His finger hit a button, and the program she had recorded last night started to play. "I was afraid I'd miss it. We can watch it together, if you like?"

The last guy she'd gone out with was intimidated by her knowledge of sports and didn't understand her love of mixed martial arts. With Jasper, she was finding out more and more, and he seemed to accept her for who she was.

"I'd like that." Like a move from a corny movie, Jasper tossed the remote on the couch, stretched, and leaned his arm across the back of the couch. Right behind her.

Jackie shook her head, smiled, and settled into the soft leather. She didn't mind him getting closer at all. As much as she tried, she'd thrown in the towel and waved the white flag. She couldn't say no to his advances anymore, even if it was only for a short while. Her life had been too lonely for too long.

In no time at all, darkness seemed to fall. They took a break from the program to eat pizza that Jasper had had delivered. Talking, drinking, and eating with someone handsome and charming was much more appealing than eating alone in her apartment. Even if it did have a better view.

They had more things in common than she thought. Onions on pizzas was one of them. A fondness for books, sports, and a dislike for science fiction were just some of the things she discovered they shared. As the evening wore on, they moved closer until there was no space between them at all. Her left side pressed up against his right. The warmth of his body eased her fears and made her feel safer than she'd felt in years.

Three wine coolers and many hours of TV later, her head drifted back onto his shoulder. That spicy aftershave he wore drew her even more. He felt safe and comforting, like she'd come home for the first time in a long time. So much so that Jackie drifted off to sleep.

Heat warmed her face, and Jackie lifted her hand to block the bright rays from the sun. Yawning and stretching, she rolled over toward the source of the light. The patio doors had curtains, but just the sheers were in place. Patio doors? She gazed around the room and sat up on the bed. Not her bed!

Jackie threw off the blanket. She was still in the same clothes, and only her shoes had been removed. There was a dent in the pillow next to hers, but she lay on top of the covers with just a blanket over top. Looking around the room, it dawned on her that she was in Jasper's bed. It was the only room he hadn't showed her last night. Because, in his words, that would mean she was staying the night. Well, it was morning, and she was still here.

It was similar to the rest of the place. Neat, orderly, and lacking in feminine touches. A few workout clothes were draped over a chair, and a pair of barbells sat in a corner. The little bit of the closet she could see boasted many of the nice suits she'd seen him wear. It was probably bursting with more of his high-end designer clothes. There was a copy of a popular bestselling western on the table nearest her. The man didn't come across as a cowboy kind of guy, but there it sat, on the table next to where she had ended up. Had he given her "his side" of the bed?

Rising, she slipped on her shoes that lay nearby on the floor and visited the master bathroom. After freshening up, she caught her reflection in the mirror as she washed her hands. Her hair was the usual mess, and her makeup had faded, hopefully not all over his pillowcase. It felt oddly intimate, standing in the same place he most likely shaved every morning. That smoldering aftershave he always wore still lingered in the air. Just imagining him in the shower with water dripping off his naked body caused her cheeks to pinken.

A door closed below. She jumped, rushed back to the bed, and covered herself again with the blanket. Not that that would protect her from anything, but at least she wouldn't look like she was snooping. Jackie wasn't, but having been a reporter, he assumed she was the big snooper in the world. It wasn't like she'd gone through any of his drawers, and truth be told, that thought never even entered her mind, but it should have. Jasper wasn't part of any kind of investigation, and she had every intention on keeping it that way.

Footsteps jogged up the stairs, and the bedroom door opened. Jasper entered, carrying a big bag of what smelled like breakfast and a carry tray of coffee.

"I'm not much of a cook, and the coffee shop you love isn't open yet. I got these at the gas station. I love 'em, so I was hoping you would too."

He pushed the book on the table aside and placed the bag there. The smell of sausage, egg, and croissants from Kwik Trip brought her fully awake. Also in the bag was a little bouquet of flowers that she also recognized from her favorite gas station. He handed them to her, and she inhaled the sweet scent.

"I love everything. Thank you." It was the truth. He always seemed to know what she liked, wanted, or needed. This was a good thing but also bad. Every day, she was falling more and more for this man. A made man. The same kind of man that killed her mom and dad.

Chapter Sixteen

Jasper

Jasper studied her from the chair he'd pulled near the bed. The sight of Jackie in his bed was something he never dreamed would happen. Granted, she was on top of the covers and not below him, but baby steps, as they say. Slowly but surely, it appeared she was succumbing to his charms. Never before had he had to work so hard to get a girl, but then things worth having didn't come easy. She was worth it. He felt it in his gut that this woman was the one.

Jackie thought they were total opposites, but they were meant to be together. How did he know this? Who knew? Love couldn't be explained. Love? Well, maybe that was getting a bit too far ahead, but what else made a man get out of bed early on Sunday morning and drive around town trying to find flowers and food?

"You look beautiful." Her hair was a mess, her clothes were wrinkled, but she had never looked prettier. It made her even more real, more appealing. More his.

"Wow, drinking already." She tried to smooth the unruly red waves with her hands.

"No. The thing is, girls think guys like them when they're all dressed up and wearing a ton of makeup." He reached for her hands to untangle them from her hair. "We like you best when you're just being you. Now eat."

The woman in front of him took the last bite of the sandwich. "These really are good." Her eyes went wide, and she quickly drew a napkin to her mouth, obviously embarrassed about talking with her mouth full. "And the cappuccino is also. Thank you again."

"My pleasure. It meant a lot to my grandfather to have you there." He took a bite of his and added, "And to me also." The smile he gave her came straight from the heart. How fun it would be to sit and find humor in simple moments like this. Jasper finished chewing and added, "And it means a lot of me to have you here." There, he said it. Was it hot in here, or was it just the coffee? He pulled his shirt away from his chest.

"That reminds me. How did I get here?" Jackie patted the bed she was sitting on.

"Don't you remember? I invited you over, and because you couldn't resist me, you agreed to come. We watched the fights together."

She rolled her eyes. "I know that part. I meant how did I end up in your bed?" Her finger pressed into the mattress.

"Easy. You fell asleep, and I carried you up here.

I couldn't let you sleep on the couch." He took another sip of his drink. "It's not very comfortable."

"I see, and where did you sleep?" Her left eyebrow raised.

It was his turn to point. "Right there. Like I said, the couch isn't very comfortable, but I swear on my mother's grave, except for carrying you here and taking off your shoes, I never laid a hand on you." He shrugged. "Not that I didn't want to, but it wouldn't have been the gentlemanly thing to do."

"And, of course, you are gentleman." She gazed up from the lid of her cup. A little foam touched her lip, and her tongue darted out to lick it off.

"I'm trying to be, but if you keep looking at me like that, I'm bound to do some very ungentlemanly things to you."

Jackie laughed, threw the blanket off, and placed her feet on the floor. "We wouldn't want that to happen now, would we?"

"I definitely wouldn't mind." He dropped a napkin into his lap to cover up just how much he did.

"I'd better get going. I'm sure you have things to do today."

"Yeah, I do."

Jackie frowned.

"I was really hoping to spend the day with you." That brought the glow back to her cheeks.

"Doing what?" She hesitated.

"Well, since you're new to the wine business, I thought I'd take you on a tour of one of the oldest wineries in the state, in the whole country, actually."

"I'd like that." Her shoulder relaxed. "Do I have time to go home and change?"

"Of course you do." He reached for her hand, and they both rose at the same time. This time, he couldn't help pulling her closer. "But if you don't want me to kiss you, speak up now."

Jackie didn't say a word, and he pulled her into his arms. She just gazed up at him with those big brown eyes that seemed to melt his heart. He lowered his mouth to hers. Her scent was becoming something familiar and something he yearned for, even when she wasn't around. Her lips were soft and eager, and he couldn't help delighting in everything she offered. He could drown in her. He *was* drowning in her. She had to say yes to him or he'd be lost. Drifting aimlessly in search of someone who wasn't her.

Her body pushed closer to his. There was no way she wouldn't be able to feel his desire for her, hard-pressed against her belly. God, he wanted his woman. His tongue explored her mouth, and with a moan, he finally lifted his head. "If we don't leave now, I don't think I'll be able to let you go." His voice was heady and deep.

"Then I'd better get going because I need a shower and to change." Her lips were swollen, and her face was flushed. Good, she was just as affected by the kiss as he was.

"Do you want me to drive you?" She stepped back, and the room instantly felt colder. He'd never be able to enter this room again without picturing her there.

"No. I'd better take my car since it's still parked

out front." She started for the door. "Do you want to pick me up, say, in an hour?"

"Sure. But wait." He picked up the flowers he'd bought for her and presented them to her.

"Thanks again." She kissed his cheek and took the bouquet. "You really are sweet."

"I know." He winked. "Just don't tell anybody."

A couple of hours later, they drove up the hilly driveway of the Wollersheim Winery. It was still early in the season, but from photos she'd seen, the place would soon be brimming with flowers and beautiful greenery when the weather turned warmer.

"It's gorgeous." Jackie shaded her face from the sun as she took in all the old and new buildings that seemed to fit so well with the surrounding landscape. Walking up to the historic building, a large oak tree had fallen over but was still left where it had landed. They had to duck under the fractured limb to continue on the sidewalk. There was a plaque stating that even though the vintage oak had fallen in a storm, it was still alive. It was too precious to the heritage of the place to let it go, so they left it where it fell to keep it thriving and growing.

"Grandfather would like that story." Jasper took her hand in his and led her to the gift shop area. He purchased two tickets for the tour. If the guys could see him now, he'd be getting the razzing of a lifetime. Jasper was never the forceful, in your face kind of guy. He never thought about doing things like this to make a woman happy before, but he'd be equally content doing it forever if it made this woman his. Funny how things changed when one

161

fell in love. He stopped short when the l-word popped into his mind again. Jackie drew his attention to some chairs made from old wine barrels.

"Maybe Dominic could make something like this." She rubbed her hand along the smooth surface.

Lucky chair!

"His taste runs more toward gun racks or knife holders, but I'm sure he could figure out something." Jasper laughed, but he could totally see Dom making something like this.

The tour started in the oldest part of the winery, which was built back in 1858. The top floor of the three-story building used to be a dance hall but was currently used for parties and events, the main floor was an old carriage house, and the bottom was the wine cellar, which held the wine aging in barrels. After a short video, they toured some of the vineyard outside.

They were both surprised to find out that the original owner Agoston Haraszthy first planted grapes back in the 1840s. He sold the place to his manager and moved to California, where he become known as the father of California wine making. After a very harsh winter in 1899, the place became a farm for many years.

The Wollersheims purchased the place back in the '70s and created faster-growing grapes that could survive in a colder climate. They had owned and operated it ever since. Somewhere along the tour, they held hands. It just happened naturally, as if they both reached for each other at the same moment.

The tour concluded with a tasting, then they trekked over to the next building. No longer satisfied with just holding hands, Jasper looped his arm around her waist and pulled her close. "Are you having fun?"

She looked up at him. "I am." The sun brought out a few freckles on her nose. "Thank you for bringing me here."

"My pleasure." He enjoyed it just as much as she seemed to.

"I didn't know you were a wine person." They walked up the stairs to the distillery.

"I'm not, but I am looking forward to visiting this building." The Wollersheims also made brandy, gin, vermouth, and even absinthe. A sales person later explained that a law left over from the Prohibition era had to be overturned so they could have a distillery and a winery at the same location.

"I'll take wine over the others any day, but a Brandy Alexander does sound good." She eyed the selection of drinks offered.

"Your wish is my command." Jasper gave the bartender her order and added a glass of apple brandy for himself. When they were ready, he grabbed both drinks and followed Jackie to a table.

"I can't believe you've never been here before." Jasper leaned closer as Jackie sipped her drink.

"I haven't done too much since I moved to Genoa. I guess, for some reason, I never thought I would stay. I'm afraid I didn't strike up many relationships or do too many things."

"Really? Why wouldn't you want to stay?"

"I don't know." She shrugged her shoulder. "I guess I didn't know if I'd like small town living."

"Is that why you turned me down when I asked you out last fall?" He had to know.

"Maybe, but I also had heard rumors about Stephanie's book being true to life and that some of the people surrounding her may have been involved with the mob."

"And now what do you think?" Jasper held his breath.

"I think this is so good." She nodded toward the drink.

"That's not what I meant."

"But it is really, really good." The woman avoided the question.

"If I poured that over my body, would you lick me?" He joked but was also considering it.

Jackie put a napkin to her mouth, fighting back a laugh.

"Jasper? Is that you?" a voice from behind asked, and they both turned toward it.

It was Connie. He stood up to greet her.

"Connie." Jasper placed a hand on her shoulder. "I've been thinking about you. How are you?" He dropped his hand to his side.

"Wonderful, thanks to you." The woman looked much better than the last time he'd seen her. The bruises had faded, and there was a lift in her step. Connie glanced at Jackie.

"Ah, Connie, this is my friend Jackie." His date stood, greeted, and shook hands with the newcomer before sitting back down.

"It's nice to meet you. How do you know

Jasper?" For the first time that day, Jasper hesitated. It was a simple question, but was it the reporter in her resurfacing? He shouldn't have had trust issues, but it was second nature for him to always be on guard.

"He helped me with a very difficult situation." Connie hugged him, and his face heated. "I still can't thank you enough. You saved my life."

Jasper brushed it off as best he could. "What are you doing here? Do you want to join us?" He motioned to the table, and she shook her head.

"No. I can't stay. I was in the neighborhood and thought I'd stop in and buy something special to celebrate with."

"Is everything going all right with your husband's estate?" He couldn't help noticing Jackie's eyes widening at that question.

"Yes, yes, couldn't be better. I should be getting the settlement soon."

"I'm glad to hear that." Jasper saluted her with his glass. "If there is anything else you need, just let me know."

"And the same goes to you also. Thanks again, Jasper." She briefly laid a hand on his shoulder before turning to Jackie. "It was nice meeting you."

They watched as Connie bought a bottle of apple brandy and practically danced out the door.

"Did I hear you right? Her husband just died?" Her mouth remained opened. "She doesn't seem too upset about it."

"He was a bad man. The worst. And he physically abused her." Jasper shifted the glass back and forth between his fingers on the table.

"That's horrible." She frowned.

"At least she'll get a big check from the life insurance policy to start over." He took a drink. The gold-colored liquid went down smoothly.

"How did he die?" Jackie tilted her head, and her lower lip pouted.

It was now or never. "I killed him," Jasper replied.

Chapter Seventeen

Jackie

Things went a little south after her "date" confessed to killing someone. Sure, the husband was a bastard. That was obvious from the blissful and appreciative reaction from the non-grieving widow, but still. They'd made small talk the rest of the day, and Jasper appeared a bit shocked by her quietness. That was the only way to describe it. She was numb. This whole situation had gotten out of hand, and there didn't seem to be a way out of it.

Jasper was non-apologetic and had explained everything in nauseating detail about what had taken place. Starting with Connie's bruised face and ending with her husband crushed under a truck. It didn't seem to faze him in the least as to what he'd done, but when he was raised that way, why would it? Jasper felt he was justified in doing what he had done, and Connie did also. It was a conundrum and something that she'd never expected to hear about.

Somewhere between the gifts and the Brandy

Alexander, she'd developed feelings for the man—deep, I'm-falling-for-the-guy kind of feelings. It wasn't infatuation, as that was short lived. She could see her being with Jasper for the long haul. And as for lust, that wasn't what she was experiencing. Not experiencing lust? Well, maybe a little. Actually, a lot, but not just a one-time thing. They could spend lazy Sunday mornings together for the rest of her life, and she'd be happy as could be. She ran her fingers through her hair and plopped her elbows onto her desk. Yes, she was attracted to him, there was no doubt about it, but that didn't mean it was smart to act on it.

"Jackie." The chair in front of her desk was suddenly pulled back, and Madison sat down. "Jackie?"

"Huh?" Her head throbbed, but it had nothing to do with the drinks she'd had the day before. No, it was because she'd tossed and turned all night thinking about a brown-eyed bad boy with perfect hair who killed husbands who beat their wives.

"Are you all right? I've been calling your name for thirty seconds or more, and you never looked up."

Jackie sat back in her chair and took a deep breath. "Sorry. I'm fine. Just have a lot on my mind."

"Me too." She frowned.

"What's wrong?" It seemed odd that Madison would be upset about anything. She was the most positive person Jackie had met in a long time.

"Do you like kids?" That was the last thing she expected her to ask.

"Ah, I guess so. Doesn't everyone?"

"Well, yes. I didn't mean it that way. It's just that, since Valentina had a baby, I've been getting a lot of not-so-subtle hints about when Roman and I will start a family."

"I can imagine so. When you're single, everyone asks when you're going to get married, and when you get married, everyone asks when you're going to have kids." It was the circle of life.

"I know. Right?" There was a smile on Madison's face, but it appeared that the subject weighed heavily on her mind.

"Do you not want kids?" Jackie hated to ask, but something was definitely wrong.

"There has to be an heir for the family. Roman would be crushed if we didn't. Heck, it might even be cause for divorce." The question wasn't answered.

"What do you want?" Jackie folded her arms across her chest.

"Honestly?" Madison mirrored her by also crossing her arms in front of her.

"Yes, that would be a good start." It was nice to see the tables turned after all the pressure Maddy had placed on her to get out and date.

"I do want kids, but to tell the truth, I'm scared to death."

"Of what?" This seemed to be an odd topic of conversation to be having with her boss, but in the short time they'd worked together, they'd become close, and they definitely had a very non-traditional boss/employee relationship.

"Everything. What if I do something wrong? The

whole pregnancy thing scares the heck out of me, not to mention giving birth." She shivered. "I faint at a paper cut, and the whole breast feeding, diaper changing…ugh, I don't even know what they eat."

Trying not to laugh, Jackie interrupted her. "I'm pretty sure every new mother feels the same way. It's a learning experience. The wonderful thing is you have a good friend that just had a baby, and I'm sure she would be more than happy to help you with anything and everything along the way."

"I know. I'm just being silly." Maddy rolled her eyes. "But I just don't want to disappoint Roman. He demands perfection in everything."

"It's never silly to be worried about the unknown, but from what I've seen and heard, Roman adores you." It was said that she was the only one he would bend his will to.

"Thanks. I know what I need to do. I just wanted to bounce my thoughts off someone. Everyone has insecurities, and this is mine." That seemed to put her more at ease. "Now, what were you pondering when I barged in like a crazy person?"

"It's nothing." The last thing she wanted to do was talk about her love life with her boss, but in a way, wasn't that what they had just finished discussing? Making babies?

"Does it involve a tall, dark, and handsome guy named Jasper?" Maddy tucked her foot under the leg on the chair.

"Unfortunately, yes." Jackie twirled a pen between her fingers.

"I though you two were starting to get along?"

"We are…were." She tossed the pen on the desk.

"I don't know. I'm so confused, and this whole thing about being committed so early in the relationship is messed up. Who dates like this?"

"Want to talk about it?" The edges of Madison's mouth turned up. It was now her turn to be the voice of reason. Hopefully.

"Yes, I do. Don't take this the wrong way, but how do you look the other way with what these guys do?"

Maddy frowned. "I wouldn't say that I look the other way, as that would make me spineless. When I first met Roman, I wanted nothing to do with him, in much the same way you were, and now are, with Jasper. Right after we met, I was kidnapped by a man whose fiancé I had convinced not to go through with the wedding. He was an abuser, and it was only going to get worse. If Roman and his men hadn't have saved me, I know I wouldn't be alive today. He rescued me but ended up shooting that man in the head." This time, it was Madison who let out a deep breath. "Right in front of me."

"Oh my God." Jackie couldn't believe it. "How do you overcome seeing something like that? Unsee something like that?"

"By realizing that, sometimes, those who we think of as bad are who save us from those who are worse." Madison looked her right in the eyes.

Jackie let that last comment simmer on the front burner of her brain. Jasper had saved Connie from what sounded like a brutal, early death from her husband. Madison then went on to tell other stories of how Valentina was saved from a serial killer, Stephanie was saved from an arranged marriage with a horrible human trafficker, and it went on and on. "But what about other illegal activities? Aren't you afraid they might all end up in jail someday?"

"Any one of us could end up in jail for doing something that we never intended to happen. Life is risky, and we're trying to move the family into more legit businesses, but that way of life is slow to change." Madison put both feet on the floor. "What I'm saying is life is short, so follow your heart. If you want Jasper, go for it. He's a great guy who also seems to be head over heels for you. Don't let someone else take what you want or that little voice in your head tell you that you can't have it."

If only it were that easy. It suddenly dawned on her that she did want Jasper. He'd been a spark that'd been lit back in the fall when they'd first met. A few weeks ago, it simmered with the first touch of his hand when they'd been introduced on the job. Now it was a blaze with promises of a future and more. Jackie wanted him with a flame that couldn't be put out, no matter how much she tried to extinguish it.

Alain knocked on her opened door. He held a couple packages in his arms.

"These are for you." He set them on the desk and left.

Madison rubbed her hands together. "What did he send you today?"

"Who?" She had an idea but didn't want to hope. They hadn't left on good terms last night. She'd been uneasy, and he'd been on edge.

"Jasper, of course. Do you have anyone else sending you things every day?" her boss teased.

"Well, no, but I didn't want to assume." There were two packages.

The first one she opened contained chocolate. "To sweeten you up," it said. Jackie laughed as he always said she was sweet enough. The next contained a bottle of wine from the Wollersheim Winery. It was Blushing Gold. He'd remember her favorite one from the tasting the day before. For so long, she'd tried to prove that he was just a player and only interested in one thing, yet he'd never done anything to warrant that. He'd been persistent but not threatening. He'd been caring and tender with her when there was obviously a dark side to his personality. He killed people! It didn't get any darker than that.

Did she have that same blackness? Something inside her that wouldn't stop until those responsible were dead? She had no right to judge him for what he was, or was raised to be, any more than she. Jackie wanted those responsible for her parents' death dead, even if she had to pull the trigger with her own finger.

Madison picked up the bottle and read the label. "I like how they do the labels with the pairings and sweetness level. We should do something like that." Madison put it back down and peeked over the desk. "What's in the last box?"

"What? Oh, I didn't even see that." There was a small one similar to the ones the jewelry had come in. Opening it, she expected to see another piece of the collection. It was a Brighton, but instead of being a piece of jewelry, it was a key chain, and there was a key attached.

"A key? What's it for?" Madison took it from her hand and oohed and aahed. "It's a Brighton again. Love their stuff. Is there a note?"

"Yes. Here it is." Jackie unfolded the paper. "It says…" She cleared her throat, and the paper shook in her hand. "'You already have the key to my heart. Now you have the key to my home.'"

Madison swooned and clutched her hands over her heart. "What are you going to do?"

"I'm not sure." Jackie sat back in her chair. "I guess I'll have to follow what my heart says."

"And is that with Jasper?" Madison wiggled her eyebrows.

"I've been trying to resist him but failing miserably. It might be time to jump in with both feet and see where it leads."

"I'm so happy for you," she gushed.

"Thanks, but nothing is for certain." Only time would tell that.

"I know, but I would love it if you became part of the family. I already feel that you are. We just need to make it official." Madison rose, came around the desk, and gave her a quick hug. "I'd better get going. I've got a lot of work to do."

"Okay, see you later." Jackie walked to her window as Madison left the room. There was a lot to think about.

Everything that surrounded the Caponellis seemed to be about oaths, commitments, and honor, it would seem, but could she really do it? Did she really see Jasper and her in love forever? Sitting, holding hands as their grandchildren looked through old photo albums like they'd done at Frankie's

174

house? Would they even have photo albums in the future? Okay, now her mind was just rambling and avoiding the question altogether.

Did she care for Jasper?

Yes.

Could she see herself with him forever?

Yes.

Could see find her way to see past some of the things he'd done and would do in the name of the mob? It would appear so, if she was going to be in a long-term relationship. That would mean staying in Genoa, which she hadn't plan on doing, but the place was growing on her and quickly feeling like home. Just like Jasper was starting to feel like home.

There was only one problem. When he found out her real reason for being here, would he still want her?

Chapter Eighteen

Jasper

A serious relationship was a new thing to him. On the one hand, it was exciting, and it gave him a sense of maturity. On the other, he'd never been so desperate to have a woman fall for him. After dropping off Jackie, he stopped at Dominic's to see if they had any insight. Stephanie said that best thing he could do right now was give Jackie some space. Jasper had done that, but it was killing him. As each day fell into the next, he was sure he'd lost the battle for her love. He'd given her a key, and she'd yet to use it.

The gifts he had sent Monday were to say he was still there for her and that the ball was now in her court. The wait was pushing him over the deep end. Several times, he'd gone outside, intending to drive over to her place, but stopped. Numerous times, he'd brought the phone out to call, only to throw it back onto the counter or bed. If he kept this up, he'd had to buy a new one soon.

Glancing at the screen for the hundredth time in the last few days, he cursed and shoved it into his pocket. Yesterday, he broke down and called Madison to get the lowdown, but she didn't have any news, either. At least she said she didn't. Now, he was even second guessing Maddy, and he had no reason to do that. She'd always been honest and straightforward with him.

Fuck it.

If Jackie didn't want him, he'd go back to one-night stands. It would never be the same as being with the woman you loved, but at least it wouldn't hurt so much.

"Jasper?" Arlo weaved his way to their table with a coffee cup in each hand. His buddy placed one on the table in front of him. They were at the Java Shop, and the place was packed. Unfortunately, Jackie wasn't among the crowd.

"Thanks." He needed a shot of whiskey, but coffee would have to do at this time of day.

"Grab it and go. Roman wants us at the garage."

"Why?" Jasper slid his chair back.

"Don't know. Don't care. Let's go." Arlo was his usual pissed-off self.

They left the Java Shop and were on the road in no time. Even at this time of day, the streets of Genoa were busy with tourists and the early return of wealthy lake homeowners.

Soon, they were turning up dust as they drove down the road to the old shed that they used for mob and MC business.

"Any idea what going on?" There were numerous bikes there already and a couple of the family's SUVs. The doors were shut, which was unusual. It would be hotter than hell in the metal building, so even if bad things were happening inside, the place was isolated enough that they kept the doors open to keep it cool.

"Nope, but it looks like something big." They got out of the vehicle and proceeded inside. Both were unprepared for what they were about to see.

Several of the Mayhem Tribe were there, including their president, Forge. Jasper recognized the former prospect, Square, who was now a patched-in member. He nodded, and Square returned the gesture. Roman, Dominic, and some of the other Caponelli crew were also in attendance. Arlo had been working with some new bodyguards, and they were with Roman today.

In the middle of the room were two half-naked, beaten and bloodied men tied to folding chairs. Judging by the tattoos, they were Russian mafia. But what the hell were they doing here? Both were missing all their fingernails. Jasper fought back a shudder. He could handle anything, but removing fingernails still gave him the willies.

Dominic wandered over. He wore only boxer briefs, and blood was splattered across his chest. They didn't usually use Dom for interrogations, as he was the cleaner, but Roman wanted everyone to be well-versed in all duties, in case someone was not available. That might have been why he and Arlo hadn't been called over sooner. They might have been sent here to clean up this one. He'd done it with Dom several times, so that was no sweat. Heck, he wouldn't have to worry about ruining his clothes, either.

"What's with the IVs?" Arlo nodded toward the men in the chairs. Both were barely conscious, and their heads were lowered.

"They lost blood too fast and didn't talk. We needed to keep them alive longer, so we did a blood transfusion."

Arlo strode over to study the work that'd been done.

"What's the deal? Why are the Russians here?" Jasper wondered out loud. "Are they the ones that took the guns?"

"Not sure yet. Caught them by accident." Dominic picked up a screwdriver from the work table. It appeared to be the same one he'd used to stab his opponent with in a fight to the death last year.

"And?" Sometimes, Dom's lack of conversation drove him up the wall.

"They got a little rough with one of the girls who works in the club's brothel." The Tribe owned a whorehouse out in the country. "Not sure how they even got in."

"Why. Are. They. Here." Jasper's patience ran thin.

"That's what we're trying to find out, asshole." Dom pointed the tool at him.

"Dickhead." Jasper took the screwdriver from his hand and threw it back on the work table.

"You cut them too deeply," Arlo said. "If you don't want them to bleed out so fast, don't go so deep, and for fuck's sake, avoid the arteries. Remind me to get you an anatomy book."

"Since when are you a fucking doctor?" Dom placed his fists on his hips. "You know I don't like this shit. I like dealing with the ones who don't talk back."

Jasper watched the battle between the two and rolled his eyes. Over the heads of the crowd, he could see Roman in deep conversation with Forge. Something was up, but he still had no clue.

"Dammit, if you want something done right, you have to do it yourself." Arlo slipped out of his clothes until he was wearing nothing more than Dom.

"I'm starting to feel over-dressed," Jasper joked, but neither of his companions seem to think it was funny.

"Shut the hell up." Arlo marched over to Roman. After a few words with him, Arlo went over to the Russians and slapped them awake. "Names."

Shit was about to get real, and everyone moved closer to the action, including Jasper, who now stood behind Arlo.

"Yegor and Dima," one of the Russians mumbled.

Dominic marched over and whispered in Arlo's ear. "They already said that."

"I'm starting a line of conversation. Back off."

Jasper put his hands in his pockets and enjoyed the show while his two friends battled it out. Dominic didn't usually get riled, but he still got agitated by crowds, a lingering effect from many years in an illegal fighting ring that he wasn't part of by choice.

There was also way too much testosterone in the

room right now. Everyone wanted to be the one to crack the mystery of why these men were in their territory and show who had the biggest dick.

"Why are you here?" Arlo yelled in their faces, but neither answered. One appeared incapable of speaking. His eyes rolled around in his head, and there was blood and drool coming out of his mouth. "You will be dead today." Arlo walked over to the work bench as he spoke. "You have two choices. Speak up and go quickly or remain silent and linger for hours as I…" He stopped and picked up a cheese shredder. Where the hell had that come from? It was rusty and old. Arlo glanced up, and Jasper could have heard a pin drop. "As I shred the skin from your body."

The Russian who drooled threw his chair backward and his head cracked on the concrete. He'd decided to kill himself rather than endure another moment of torture. Well, that one wasn't going to talk. Dominic jumped behind the other before he could do the same. Arlo returned to his victim's side and made a quick brush of the kitchen tool up the man's arm. His victim screamed as his skin fell off in small pieces. Blood dripped to the floor.

"Stop. Stop." The man pleaded as tears now ran from his eyes. "Stop. I'll tell you what I know." With the torture from Dominic and now from Arlo, they'd broken him. "Please. Stop."

"Speak up." Arlo slapped the man's face again. If they didn't get him talking soon, the guy might go into cardiac arrest. Jasper had seen it happen. Guys too stressed and pressed so hard that their heart exploded.

"Okay, okay," he slurred. Roman stepped in front of the man now. "We were sent from Chicago to find someone. We were stupid and ended up at the brothel instead."

"Who are you trying find?"

"Alexander." Dima spit some blood as he spoke.

"Who?" Roman demanded.

"He's the brother of my boss. The guy's *bezumnvy*. He's crazy. Alexander beat up several whores who work in our houses. Everyone looked the other way until Alex took the boss's favorite girl." The man stopped to catch his breath. "He left her body outside of town. It was a message." Jasper's gaze locked on Arlo's. This was the girl Ryan had told them about.

"What kind of message?" Arlo kicked the man's leg. "And who do you work for?"

"Fedor Dubnikov. Like I said, Alexander's crazy. He means to make the boss look weak. Cause conflict." Dima paused again. "The girl was a strike to his heart. Leaving her here in your territory was a strike to his power."

"How so?"

"Fedor wants to take over the Caponelli and Rinaldi territories. That Alexander can commit a crime on your turf and get away with it means he should be boss and not Fedor."

"The Tribe's had their eyes on you for days. You bought stolen guns just recently."

This time, it was Forge who spoke up. "We tracked down where you were staying. You've been here for weeks. Much before that girl was found."

"We were sent here before that." The story kept changing.

"Why were you here before they had you looking for Alexander?" This time, it was Roman who asked the question.

"They want to kidnap your women. We were to keep an eye on them. Learn their routines and places they go."

"What women? Who did they want to take?" Roman loosened his tie.

"Your wife, her sister, and your sister." Arlo grabbed the man by the throat, and Roman pulled him off. As hard as he tried to deny it, everyone knew Arlo had the hots for Layla, but taking any one of those women would have everyone up in arms.

"Who ordered this?" Roman remained calm, but there was no doubt his boss wanted blood. The veins on his forehead pulsed.

"I told you. The boss, Fedor Dubnikov." The guy didn't hesitate to answer now. If fact, he seemed eager to talk, but once he had nothing more to say, it was lights out.

"Where can we find him?" He stuttered some Chicago address that Roman sent off to the tech guys.

Jasper stood close as they continued the questioning. It was soon obvious that this guy didn't know much more but did finally reveal the location of the stolen guns. The fact that the two men would stop at a whorehouse belonging to a known ally of the Caponellis spoke volumes. They were idiots. Stealing guns from a motorcycle club reinforced that notion, as well.

After questioning him for ten more minutes, there was nothing left to find out. They untied Dima. He did a weak sign of the cross before Arlo easily snapped his neck.

They left the dead men where they lay as Roman gathered everyone around. "Thank you Forge and members of the tribe for bringing this to my attention. We wear different uniforms, but we are brothers underneath." Several bikers nodded, and a few cheered. "A strike at our territory is a strike on yours, as we work together here. Be vigilant. If they are coming after our women, they may be coming after yours." A few curses followed. "Thank you again, and we'll keep in touch."

Jasper stayed in the background as he witnessed members of the tribe shaking Roman's hand before they left. Soon, the loud rumble of bikes thundered outside. The shed doors were wide open now as Dominic backed his van up to the shed to gather the bodies. They'd soon be taking them to the funeral home they were connected with to incinerate the dead.

No bodies. No witnesses. No crime. No DNA.

"Do you need help, Dom?" Jasper volunteered.

"Depends. Are you going to remain quiet the whole time?" Dominic asked while wiping the blood from his body and donning a clean pair of overalls.

"Probably not."

"Then the answer is no." Dominic did allow him to assist in getting them into the van, but it was clear he'd reached his limit of social activity for the day.

After Roman finished talking to his bodyguards, he returned to speak to Arlo. "From this time forward, we need two men with Madison at all times."

"Yes, sir," Jasper spoke for them both.

"What about Layla?" Arlo wiped his hands on a towel.

"That's Rinaldi's problem. He's her father and not our responsibility."

"She's your sister-in-law." Arlo wouldn't give up. "That makes her family."

"Not in this case. If Rinaldi wants our help, he will ask for it, but she should be fine under his protection where she is." Roman placed one hand on his soldier's shoulder. "Until then, we keep an eye on our own, and that means Madison is never alone. Understood?"

"Yes, sir," they answered in unison.

"Get this shit cleaned up, and I want you two back at the winery." He pointed to Arlo and Jasper. "I've got one guy there now, but they're new. I want only the best by my wife."

After helping Dominic clean up the floor, Arlo washed up and dressed quickly. Before long, they were back on the road to town, and Dom was on the way to the crematory.

The whole thing reeked of bad news. For right now, things were kept on the down low, but soon, the Russians would notice two of their men were missing in Caponelli territory and then what? Clearly, Arlo was worried about Layla. He had a white-knuckle death grip on the steering wheel.

"You know everyone's going to call you 'the shredder' now." Jasper tried to lighten the mood.

"I don't give a shit. If anyone harms a hair on Layla or Madison's head, I will tear them apart, piece by piece."

"We all will." They drove into the winery parking lot, but it was pretty bare. His heart dropped when he noticed Jackie's car was no longer there. He missed her, but she'd be safer if she wasn't mixed up with him. Never would he forgive himself if something happened to her because of who and what he was.

But it wasn't up to him. He'd left it to her, and she had one more day to decide. He wasn't waiting any longer.

Chapter Nineteen

Jackie

Her head throbbed. So much so that she'd asked to leave work early. It was just too much to deal with in such a short time. Starting a new job was stressful enough without a larger-than-life handsome man pressuring you to make a lifetime decision in less than a week.

Jackie glanced at the new watch on her wrist. It was the latest gift. A Brighton silver-plated watch with the infinity design and Swarovski crystals. The latest in the collection arrived with a note saying time was running out.

It was. She was running out of time to find her parents' murderers and running out of time with Jasper. He was never supposed to have been a part of this, but now he was front and center.

The warm water ran down her face. The shower had helped ease the pain in her head but not the one in her heart. If she left without seeing where things went with Jasper, it could be the biggest regret of her life. The more she stewed over it, the more she wanted to be with him, even if it was for just a short time.

Toweling off, Jackie took a good long look in the mirror. He seemed to see something in her that others didn't. Somewhere between the watch and the shower, the decision had been made. Jackie just didn't want to admit it, but she had.

Dressing quickly in a matching pink bra and pants, a sundress, and all the jewelry he'd given her, Jackie slipped on a pair of high-heeled sandals. As much as she tried to fight it, she wanted to be with Jasper. Wanted to feel love, even if it wouldn't last. The key he'd given her lay on the table by her bed. Clutching it to her heart, she found her car keys and proceeded out the door.

Her confidence wavered when Jasper wasn't there when she arrived. Since he'd given her the key, Jackie used it to let herself in. Her heels clicked on the floor as she roamed around the empty space wringing her hands. Her throat was dry, and she opened the fridge for something to drink. An open bottle of wine seemed like a good choice, and she chugged it straight from the bottle. So much for being ladylike, but it worked. The liquid warmed her, and she took a second drink. Visiting the winery together was a romantic date she'd never forget. It was also where she'd learned he'd killed someone.

Jackie jumped when the sound of a car door slamming outside brought her back to the present. She risked one more sip, replaced the cork, and put the bottle back where she'd found it. From the window, she saw him turn toward her car but couldn't see his face. The doorknob wiggled as he put the key in. Wringing her hands, she wondered what his reaction to seeing her in his place would be. They had really not talked all week.

Jasper entered and shut the door behind him. Spying her across the room, his mouth lifted in a flirty smirk. "I hope this means you're mine." He tossed his keys and phone on the counter and started her way.

Her knees shook as she took a step closer. "I'm really not sure what this means. I just know I couldn't go any longer without being with you." With trembling fingers, she unzipped the dress and let it fall to the floor. Jasper stopped. His eyes widened as his gaze drifted slowly from the tips of her toes to her eyes. Her hand fluttered to the necklace around her neck—the one he had given her. It seemed weird, but it felt like he possessed her now. Not because of the gifts but because of the feelings and thought behind them. He wanted forever. She wanted him, even if it was for just one night.

Jasper took off his jacket and laid it across the back of a chair. He loosened his tie and tossed that aside. Who knew unbuttoning the cuffs of his shirt could be so sexy, but she'd practically melted right on the spot. Was this his way of making her wait as he had been waiting for her? She licked her lips as he removed his shirt, and it joined the jacket. His brown eyes never left hers. Jasper took another step. So near that the scent of his musky aftershave tickled her nose. Jackie reached to put her hand on

189

his hair-roughened chest, but he grabbed it in his. A fierce expression crossed his face before being replaced with one full of love and what could only be called adoration.

"I've been waiting a lifetime for you." His voice was low and breathy. "I just didn't know it until now."

If she'd been worried about him being a player before, all those doubts were gone. His eyes said even more than his words did. He wanted her, he needed her, he loved her, and she felt the same way.

Jasper pulled her to his chest. The touch of his skin against hers was smooth and warm. He'd kissed her before, but when his lips met hers this time, it was different. Possessive, commanding, and making her knees weak. His arm wrapped around her waist to hold her in place. Her breasts pressed up against his hard pecs. With the other hand, he weaved his fingers through her hair, deepening the assault on her lips.

He tasted of coffee and sweets, two of her favorite things. It was a kiss of a lifetime. A promise of things to come. A promise of forever. A groan escaped her mouth when his lips left hers. "You all right?" His eyes searched hers.

"Never better." It was true. Tomorrow be damned. Tonight, she would live. "Your kiss made my knees weak." She stroked his ego, even if every word she said was true.

"I can fix that." Jackie squealed as he bent down and picked her up like she was light as a feather. "Are you staying with me?"

It should have been obvious, since she was

wearing next to nothing, but he asked again, "Are you saying you're mine?"

"Yes." For how long was anyone's guess, but for now, she was exactly where she wanted to be. He kissed her again and carried her to the bedroom where he placed her on the bed. Shyness kicked in, and she reached for a pillow. Jasper took it out of her hands and placed it to the side.

"Never hide. You're so beautiful to me. The most beautiful one in the world." His fingers touched the necklace he'd given her. "Forever and always. Some men might shower women with diamonds and money, but to me, words and actions mean more."

"I don't need diamonds. Words and action are what counts." Truthfully, Jackie never cared for the overpriced rocks. Jasper had been more thoughtful and romantic than any solitaire ever could be.

"Someday, I'll give you a diamond." The mattress lowered as he put one knee down and joined her on the bed. "Unless you'd rather have something else."

"The only thing I want is you." The last thing she wanted to think about now was wedding rings and promises.

"You have me." He nuzzled her neck with kisses that tickled and teased; Jasper's hands caressed her skin raising good bumps with every stroke. "Am I really the only woman to ever be in this bed?" She had to know.

Jasper raised his gaze to hers. "I swear. The first, only, and last." Her heart soared. It was almost hard to breathe, it felt so full. Jackie traced a finger along his jaw. It was rough and scratchy with a five o'clock shadow, but she yearned to feel that surface against every part of her body.

"Don't stop now." Her palm cupped his cheek before moving to his soft, thick hair.

"I don't plan on it." His assault on her lips continued where they left off in the living room. Jasper fingers easily unhooked her bra, and he cupped her breasts in his palms. "Beautiful. Just beautiful."

She arched her back off the bed as Jasper teased first one nipple and then the next in his mouth. Jasper dropped kisses between her breasts before working his way down her stomach. Reaching her panties, he slowly slid them down her legs.

With a devilish glint to his eyes, Jasper dropped between her thighs and began to kiss and tease. "I can't take it anymore." Jackie pulled him up by the hair to stop. "Don't make me wait any longer. We have all night to explore, but for now," she placed her arms tightly around his back, "make me yours."

"Anything you say, Angel." Jasper positioned himself between her thighs then stopped. "Shouldn't we be having that awkward conversation about safe sex and condoms right now?"

"Jasper!" The guy drove her crazy in more ways than one. "I'm clean and on birth control."

"I am too." Yet he stalled again. Was something wrong? Had he changed his mind?

"Jasper, what are you waiting for?" It was too much to take. She was primed and ready to go, and now he had taken his foot off the gas.

"As much as I want to go fast, I don't want the

moment to fade too quickly," he admitted, and she felt a tear form in her eye.

Jasper was sweet. Jasper was sexy. And when he finally entered her, slowly, Jasper was finally hers.

Chapter Twenty

Jackie

Snuggling closer to the warm body behind her, Jackie yawned.

"Good morning, Angel." Jasper kissed her shoulder and drew her close, his arm tight across her chest and nestled between her breasts. It wouldn't be surprising if she was rosy from end to end with whisker burns from his chin. How many times had they made love last night? Three. No, four. Two times in bed, once in the bathroom, their eyes meeting in the mirror as he bent her over the sink, oh, and then in the kitchen when they got hungry. Her cheeks burned thinking about him loving her with his mouth on the top of the kitchen counter.

Jasper was her dream come true. A romantic, gorgeous man who seemed to want no one but her. He was also a self-admitted killer. She pushed that fact out of her mind for the time being.

"Morning." She entwined her fingers with his.

Jasper's phone buzzed, and he cursed. "Excuse me."

Her skin chilled when it lost contact with his, but as soon as he grabbed his cell, he enveloped her in his arms again. "Yeah?" he answered it.

It was a male voice on the other end, but she couldn't hear what they said.

"Okay, I'll be there as soon as I can." He ended the call and tossed it on the bed. "There's nothing I would rather do than spend the rest of the day in bed with you, but I've got to go."

"Work?" She rolled over to face him.

"Yeah, and I'm not sure how long it will take. Could be all day."

Her gaze lowered to his lips, and she dropped a kiss there. "It's all right. I should get home anyway. I've got laundry piling up."

"Bring it here. Move in here." Jasper pulled her on top of him. "Let me buy you new clothes." He laughed.

"We'll talk about that later. You have to go, and so do I." She framed his face and kissed him again. It was something she could do all day and never tire.

The man beneath her let out a groan. "I'm so sorry." He rolled her back to her side of the bed and slowly got to his feet. Damn, he was hot. Last night was a rush, but now in the daylight, she had more time to feast with her eyes. Long legged, slim waist, and tight muscles in all the spots they should be, and judging by the large erection pointing her way, he was very attracted to her. "Keep looking at me like that, and I'm going to be in big trouble for

195

being late."

"I'm going also." She dragged herself out of the bed, and he started to dress. They had clothes scattered throughout the house.

When they were finally dressed, Jasper hugged her and kissed her forehead. "I'll call you later and let you know when I'm done. We'll go out to eat or something."

"Sure. I'd like that." His phone rang again.

"Damn. I got to go. Just lock up when you leave." He looked at the screen.

"I will. You'd better go." She gently pushed him away.

Jasper rushed out the door without answering it.

Jackie sat down to slip on her shoes. This time, it was her phone that rang. It was Madison.

"Hello?" It was a Saturday. Did she want to do lunch?

"Jackie, I hate to bother you, but I have a favor to ask."

"Sure. What is it?"

"I know it's a Saturday, but I have a shipment coming in, and I can't be there to accept it."

"Do you need me to go to the winery?"

There was a sigh of relief on the other end of the line. "Yes, and you'd be a lifesaver if you did."

"Of course." Maddy gave her the name of the delivery man and the time he'd be there. Jackie had just been given a key a few days ago, in case of emergencies like this. There was a lot to do before they opened for the summer season. Plus, Madison hadn't been acting herself. She seemed tired and even teary at times. "Is everything all right?"

"Yes, Roman has to travel, and I'm going with him. Everything is fine, so don't worry."

"Okay, I'll take care of things." It was the least she could do for all that Madison had done for her.

"Thanks. Got to go." The call ended before she could say goodbye. That was odd. Jasper had to rush away, and now, so did Madison. Was it mob business? Just the thought of it put a damper on her otherwise sunny day.

Just a short time later, Jackie waited at the back entrance to sign for the delivery. It was a shipment of glassware with their new logo that would be used for wine tastings and also to sell. The driver handed her his iPad for her to sign and said his goodbye.

Jackie locked the door and decided to check emails in her office. As the laptop kicked in, she glanced around her office. This was a dream job and not one she would ever want to leave. How could she even think about leaving Genoa, now that everything was falling into place? Reading the few emails didn't take long, and now she had to find something to do the rest of the day. That hadn't been a problem before, but now, all she wanted to do was be with Jasper again. Maybe she'd take a stroll along the lake. Yeah, that would be nice. Problem solved. She grabbed her purse and left the office.

Walking through the storage area again, something felt off. Jackie stopped and looked around. There was a chill and a damp smell in the air, but what would be causing that? Glancing around, a light caught her eye. Drifting toward the source, she spied a doorway in the wall where a door shouldn't be.

"What the hell?" A lump formed in her throat. Did she really want to look at what was inside? She'd taken this job for a change of pace, some excitement, and because her days were numbered at the Globe, but that wasn't the whole truth. All along, it'd been her hope to discover something that would prove the Caponellis were involved in criminal activities, and now it was the last thing she wanted to do. Her time in Genoa had been the means to the end—find something on them and hopefully discover who'd killed her parents. She dropped her chin to her chest. Jackie didn't have a choice anymore. Some things were set in motion that couldn't be stopped. Her palms began to sweat and her heart raced.

A peek through the door showed what she feared: a hidden room. There were boxes set all over, but nothing was written on the sides. Jackie lifted a few and was shocked to see jewelry, guns, and bricks of what could only be drugs. She dropped the cover of that box as if it was hot. Looking up, the sight of what she'd recently seen on the front page of the paper was staring her right in the face. Her jaw dropped, and her head spun. It was a Picasso, the painting that'd been stolen from Rodney Studd.

"Oh, no. Oh, no." Jackie closed her eyes and took a deep breath. This was what she'd been working for and searching for ever since her parents' murder. It was right next to her, but could she really blow the whistle and ruin what she had with Jasper? Something that had just started to grow and flourish?

In a daze, Jackie closed the door but didn't shut it all the way. Hurrying back to her office, she took a seat and calmed her nerves. Her stomach was in knots. There was only one choice, and it had to be made. If she didn't make the call, she'd had to leave anyway. Her job was to discover what Roman was up to, write a story, and turn him in.

A pit low in her gut formed as she picked up her phone and punched in the numbers she'd memorized.

"Hello." The voice on the end sent a chill up her spine. He'd been there to comfort her after her parents' deaths and all the nightmares that followed. She'd been numb and just going through the motions, exactly the same way she felt now.

"Mr. Hower. It's Jackie Messina-Smith." A pencil twirled between her fingers.

"Jackie? It's been ages. What can I do for you?" The man sounded as anxious as she was. "Is everything okay?"

"I don't know if you remember, but you know the story we talked about writing? After my parents passed?" Jackie paused. "The one that would make headlines?"

"Yes." The sound of a door closing could be heard in the background. "I'm listening."

"Well, I got it. Everything we need."

"I have to have proof and nothing less." He breathed heavy on the line.

"How soon can you get here?" She closed her eyes to keep the tears from falling. Jasper thought of her as an angel, but when this was done, he would think she was the devil.

After that call ended, she placed one more to seal her fate.

***

Jasper

It was hard to concentrate when every time he thought about the last twenty-four hours, he was hard and happy.

"What's your problem?" Arlo was always gruff. At least, that's what it seemed like lately. The guy complained if someone talked too much and was bothered if they were too quiet.

"Nothing. Just trying to figure out what's going on with the Russians. The last thing we need right now is a war."

"Tell me about it." They were in the lead car, followed closely by Roman, Maddy, and their bodyguards. They'd gone to Chicago for an early meeting at Roman's father's home, where they'd met with Madison and Layla's father Bruno Rinaldi.

The Bratva had been made several strikes against Caponelli and Rinaldi businesses in Chicago recently. They'd gotten along fine, meaning no border fights in ages, but now they were showing muscle for no reason. The meeting had gone long, and they all ended up staying at the complex in the windy city for several hours. Jasper called Jackie a couple times, but she never answered. He was on the verge of driving back, but she finally texted later in the day saying everything was fine and she'd wanted to catch up on things around home.

It put him at ease when he contacted the tech guys and they verified she was at home. He was concerned. They never did find the brute that had brutally attacked a young woman, and knowing it was an unhinged Russian thug made it even more dangerous. Jasper had the tech guys implant tracking devices in all the jewelry he'd given Jackie, so it would be a good bet she'd be wearing at least one at some time or the other.

All the guys had trackers on their phones and on the phones of their women. If something went wrong, they wanted to be able to gather everyone at a moment's notice. Jasper exhaled and tapped a finger on his knee. It was late afternoon before they were on the road home, and he was anxious to get back to town.

Arlo's cell went off. He answered it then put it on speaker.

"Jasper?" It was Roman. Now what?

"Here."

"I need all of you tonight. Dom will be there also." He went on to say the time, in code, and the place they would meet. "I'll give you further info when we get there."

"Yes, sir." The last thing he wanted to do was spend a night away from Jackie, so they'd better have a good reason. "What's this about?"

"Someone double crossed the family, and we need to take care of it." Roman spoke loudly and clearly.

Arlo glanced his way, and his eyes widened.

"We'll be there, boss," Jasper answered and

ended the call.

"Do you think it's the Russians?" Arlo seemed obsessed with finding someone to beat the shit out of, and they were his new favorite target.

"Nothing would surprise me after what happened the other day."

"Do you think this means war?" Before, he would have jumped at the chance to even the score and fight, but that was before Jackie. He hated being apart from her. Hated taking unnecessary risks that might prevent him from being home at night. Just being in Chicago for a few hours had him itching to get the hell out of there and back to her.

"I don't have a fucking clue," Arlo grumbled. "But whatever needs to be done, I'll do it."

It was late evening when they drove up to the end of the tunnel that was the back way into the winery. Dominic was at the door, a somber expression on his face.

"What's up?" Jasper got out of the car and approached his friend. Arlo was close behind.

"You're not going to like it." Dom ran his fingers through his long hair before tying it up in a knot. "Shit's about to go down here tonight, and your girlfriend's involved."

Chapter Twenty-One

Jackie

Her stomach twisted, and she fought back the nausea caused by just being in the same room with the guy. All the trauma came rushing back. The phone call in the middle of the night that her parents had been murdered. Going to the morgue to identify the bodies. No one should ever have to do that. Ever. Andrew Hower was waiting for her when she showed up at the police station. He was there to help her through the whole process, whether she needed it or not. At that point in time, Jackie had no idea what she wanted, except to have her mom and dad back.

It was a mob hit, he had told her, and the police had agreed. Hower stressed that she never mention anything about what her father had been about to publish. To protect herself, he'd said. The story would stay buried, even though she had told him over and over again that she knew nothing about what it contained.

Hower met her after dark, and they parked their cars behind the main building of the winery. She'd used her key, and they entered her work place. Cold air greeted them as they entered the room Jackie wanted him to see. It matched the chill that flowed through her veins. There was no way this would end well. In fact, one of them would die today. It was a given. Maybe they both would before it was all said and done.

"And you've looked in all of these?" Hower rubbed his palms together. A virtual kid in a candy store. He opened one and pulled out a handful of diamond necklaces. Andrew replaced them and peeked in another. "Drugs, guns, jewelry. What else did you find?"

"Bags of cash, bootleg booze. Turn around and look at this." She signaled with her hand. "There's the Picasso that was reported stolen from Rodney Studd's home. That alone would put them in jail for years."

"This is amazing, Jackie." He studied the painting up close. "There are millions of dollars' worth of stuff here, and all stolen." Hower turned her way. "Have you told anyone else about this?"

She placed her hand over her heart. "What? Of course not. You said to only tell you." Everything that had accrued in the last year rushed back, and her head throbbed. Suddenly, everything with Jasper came to the surface, and her knees wobbled. Was it all worth it? Yes, but it still hurt like hell. "I could never pass up the chance to bring the person responsible for my parents' death to justice. It's all I've thought about ever since it happened." Andrew opened a few more boxes, and she risked a glance at her watch. It wouldn't be long, and all this would be over with.

He placed the lid back on one of the totes and rested his elbows on it. "You know, I've always liked you, Jackie. You have spunk, and your father would've been proud of your investigative skills. You'd make a great reporter, just like your dad."

"Thank you." Her heart raced, and it was hard to remain calm.

"Too bad you'll never get to be one." His voice echoed in the hollow room.

"What do you mean? This will be a big scoop, just like the one my dad was working on."

"Yes. It would be." Hower pulled a gun out from under his jacket. "That's why it pains me so to have to kill you."

"What?" Her mouth dropped open, and she took a step back. "What're you doing?"

"Finishing the job your father started." He motioned with the gun for her to take a seat. It was a good thing, as her legs were about to give out.

"I don't understand. Why are you doing this? Why would you shoot me? You were his friend." She sobbed.

"*Was* being the operative word." The man's whole demeanor had changed in an instant. "He made the mistake of going after someone who I was on the payroll to protect. The Russian mob pays me well, and when your father found out about their link to powerful political members, well, we had to put him down." He was a fiend and even worse than she expected.

"Put him down?" She rose. "He was my father, not a wounded animal, and what about my mother? She was innocent. They were my parents." A tear rolled down her cheek, and anger filled her blood.

"It was them," he pointed a thumb to his chest, "or me." His hard-soled shoes reverberated off the cement walls as he circled the room before coming to stand in front of her. "And now, poor little Jackie, it's your turn."

***

Jasper

True fear was foreign to him. Not knowing what was going on, except that Jackie was involved, had beads of sweat rolling down the back of his neck as they stood waiting in the damp tunnel.

All he knew was to keep his mouth shut and that Roman was in charge, but could he do nothing when the woman he loved was in danger?

It happened in a second. The man pointed a gun at Jackie. Roman and Arlo rushed the room, and Dominic had him in a choke hold. Him. Not the guy with the gun!

What the fuck?

The only thing that kept him from a full-blown meltdown was when Dominic whispered in his ear. "Don't say a word. It's a setup. She's in on it. She's not in danger."

Jackie was part of this, whatever *it* was. "Keep quiet, or she might end up getting hurt." Jasper could see what was going on as Roman and Arlo quickly disarmed a man he'd never seen before. "If I let you go, do you promise not to engage?"

Slowly, Jasper nodded, and Dom released him. "Just listen. I don't know the whole story, but that guy killed her parents."

"What?" Jasper tightened his fists. The urge to tear this man limb from limb was stronger than anything.

He watched as Arlo easily tied the man's hands behind his back and threw him onto a chair. Madison wrapped her arms around Jackie and led her to a bench to sit.

Wait a minute, Maddy is here?

Roman never involved her in family business. Both women appeared pale and shaken.

He took a step forward, and Dominic grabbed his arm. "You promised. Step back. Let Roman play this out."

Jasper cursed under his breath. "Yeah, yeah." He shook out of his grasp but stayed where he was. This was killing him, but his friend was right. Going in blind to a situation he knew nothing about was never a smart move.

"Mr. Caponelli." The man in the chair finally spoke. "We meet for the first time."

"As if we would have reason to." Roman folded his arms across his chest, a handgun held tightly in his grip. "You're a liar, a murderer, and a front for the Bratva."

"Whatever you say, but I've never killed anyone." The man avoided eye contact and glanced down at the floor.

"Hower, you no good bastard. You knew the

story Sid wrote was going to bring unwanted attention to the Russians. You reported it to them, and they put a hit on her mom and dad. You were responsible for the death of Jackie's parents, even if you didn't pull the trigger." Roman's voice roared in the windowless room. "So shut the fuck up while I tell you what's going to happen."

This time, the doomed man turned his attention to Roman, and so did everyone else.

"You will die today." Roman walked around the room as he spoke.

Jasper watched Jackie as everyone waited to hear what would happen next.

"Your reputation will die today." Roman stopped in front of the man in the chair. "Arlo and Dominic are going to take you back to a no-tell motel outside of town and hang you from the ceiling. We've already cleared out your room in town, and the tech guys have copied and erased everything on your laptop. They will soon do the same thing with your phone." Arlo plucked Hower's phone from his pocket. "Then, as you swing from the rope and take your last breath, they will download kiddy porn and other sick shit that the police will uncover. Your bank account will be emptied and be transferred to an offshore account where Jackie can do what she wishes with it." Hower's face turned white, and he slumped in the chair. It was over, and there wasn't a damn thing he could do about it.

"I don't want his blood money," Jackie hissed.

"Donate it, if you want, but it's yours. End of story." Roman was in full command of the situation. "Any last words?"

The soon-to-be-dead man remained still, and the room reverberated with the slap of Roman's hand across Hower's face. "I repeat, anything you wish to say?" Everyone turned to Jackie.

"I'm sorry for what happened to your parents, but you can't condone this." Hower whimpered. Suddenly, Arlo pulled the man to his feet. "Jackie, please, you have to save me." Dom came out for the shadows and helped drag him away. The screams from the man for help visibly shook Jackie, and Madison placed a comforting hand on her shoulder.

"I'm no better than him." Tears streamed down her face. "I'm a murderer now too."

"No." Madison knelt by her side. "You probably saved many others from losing loved ones also. You weren't the only one he did this to. The man is a swine. He had a front row seat to keep an eye out for the Bratva, and anyone who might be a threat was eliminated."

Madison had stepped into the shoes of a mob wife and was clearly the perfect one to be by Roman's side. "Do you understand?" Maddy stood now and repeated her statement again.

Jasper watched as Jackie finally lifted her head and said, "Yes." She rose and wiped her tears. "What happens next?"

"Jasper." He'd been so concerned with watching his woman, Jasper jumped when Roman called his name.

"Yeah, boss?" Walking out from where Dom and he had waited in the wings, Jackie made a move in his direction, but Roman stopped her.

"Wait." His boss held a hand up.

"Jackie, I had no idea this was going on. I would've been here for you." Jasper's heart broke just thinking about what she'd gone through. "Why didn't you tell me? Did he threaten you? Was that why he was here?"

"I brought him here. It was a trap, and I didn't want you to know." She sighed. "You were never supposed to be a part of this." Jackie shook her head, and all he could think about was running his fingers through those reddish curls as he hugged her close.

"What are you talking about?" Jasper asked.

"It started last summer. I was at a coffee shop in Chicago, and this man just sat down next to me. He gave me his card and said he represented the Caponelli family. They knew who killed my parents but couldn't prove it. The man told me if I wanted to see the guilty ones brought to justice, they needed my help." She stopped and brushed a tear from her eye. "At first, I said no. I thought it was crazy, but he was very convincing, and I agreed. Before long, everything fell into place. The job at the paper, the nice apartment on the lake. I knew those things didn't materialize by accident, but nothing else happened. I got complacent and decided I was going to give it until the end of the summer and move on." Jackie puffed out her cheeks. "Then Madison stopped in with the ad, and I knew the deal was back on. I tried to pretend it was nothing more than needing a job, but in the back of my mind, I knew this was it. The man said that, at some point, the Caponelli family here would contact me, but I was supposed to say nothing to no one, not even them. Then Madison started pushing me toward you and," her voice trailed off, "I wasn't sure I wanted to do it anymore. Too many people were going to get hurt."

"I still don't understand what this has to do with the man they just dragged out of here." Jasper shook his head. "How did he get here and why?"

"In time, I was to uncover some illegal activities going on in Genoa and report it to Hower. Tell him it was a big story and that I wanted to follow in my father's footsteps. Hower was his editor at the paper."

"Maddy and I knew about it but weren't sure how to go about getting the guy here. With your involvement with Jackie, we were able to keep her even closer to the family than if she were just an employee." Roman words dropped like a pit in his stomach. "When you had the idea for the painting, I ran with it. There's no international jewel thief coming, and the bricks of drugs are powered sugar. I would never leave that kind of merchandise here at my wife's place of business. The painting is the only thing that's hot, but I needed something stolen to make it convincing."

Jasper calmed his nerves but was on the verge of breaking. "I don't get this at all. You played me?" He pointed at Roman before turning his attention to Jackie. "And you played hard to get but then claimed to fall for me?" His jaw tensed.

"No, I didn't, and no I wasn't. I fought it as much as I could, but everyone basically set us together. I didn't want to fall for you, but I did anyway." Jasper wanted to believe her, but he still had no clue what the truth was.

"Yes, and that's what brings me to the next problem we have to deal with," Roman interrupted. "Maddy, come here." She did as told and wrapped her arms around his waist.

"What do you need me to do?" Jasper itched to get the hell out of here and fast. He needed time to sort things through, and if it wasn't too late, he'd love to get a few punches in on the bastard Hower before he was killed.

"You can help me decide which one of you I should kill." Roman now had a gun in each hand. One pointed one at him and one toward Jackie.

"Whoa." Jasper put his hands up. "I knew nothing about this."

Jackie appeared just as shocked as he was. Well, good for her. The other surprising thing was that Maddy just stood there, glancing back and forth between the two of them.

"You see, that's the problem. Even though I set this up, you should have known what was going on, Jasper. You got involved with a woman who was not part of the family. You shared secrets. You put her and us at risk." It was true. He'd been careless over a woman. A woman whom he loved.

Well, *thought* he loved. Now, he wasn't so sure.

"The last thing I would ever do is put the organization at risk, and I would die for you. You know that is true."

"But given a choice, which would you pick?" Roman put one gun away but pointed the remaining one back and forth between Jackie and Jasper "Her or us?"

Jasper closed his eyes. This was a nightmare. As angry at and hurt as he was by Jackie, he still loved her. It was true. "Neither," he finally admitted. "I would die for both. Shoot me, if you have to." He held up his hands. "I'm over this shit."

"No. No. No." Jackie raced over to his side. "Jasper was never part of this. You can't kill him."

"Are you saying you would die for him, as well?" Roman held the gun in their direction. He was testing them both.

"This is crazy. No one needs to die," Jackie pleaded.

"No, they don't. But if I had to pick one of you, who would it be?" Roman insisted.

Madison remained quiet by her husband's side.

"Jasper has all of you. You're his family. You need him, and he needs you. I have no one left, no family. I couldn't live with the thought that he died because of me." Jackie stepped in front of him. She'd chosen him, and she'd chosen to die for him. His heart soared and dropped, all at the same time.

Chapter Twenty-Two

Jasper

"That's where you're mistaken, Jackie. We're your family. Your father was a distant relative of my father's," Roman addressed Jackie. "While he worked on that expose, he contacted us about the information he'd found out about the Russians. Sid made us promise to take you in if anything ever happened to him, and in exchange, he gave us all the goods that he found first. That's why, after they passed, I had my man contact you," Roman explained.

"None of that matters. I still turned you in to get Hower and made the call to the number the guy gave me. What if someone had gotten killed?" Jackie argued. "I'd never forgive myself. I just called and didn't think."

"We set you up to do this, and Madison helped me." Roman motioned between the two of them, while Maddy smiled and leaned her head against her husband's shoulder. "You're a smart girl. You had to know we were involved and that nothing would happen."

"Don't you remember? I asked you to stop here to help the delivery man. We left the door open for you. You played right into our hands and did everything we wanted you to do."

"But…" Jackie wouldn't give up.

"Believe me, I know everything that goes on in this town. Most often, even before it happens," Roman reassured her. "You helped us, and that's that."

Jasper remained silent as he listened to more of the story. His mind was in turmoil. He'd been played, a chess piece that they'd all moved around the board to win the game, no matter the cost. He felt like a fool. A love-sick fool. For the first time in his life, he'd given his all to a woman, only to be crushed and tossed aside like day-old bread.

What could only be called fear popped out of nowhere. Anxiety ran through his veins. Just mere minutes ago, he'd been ready to die for Jackie. Now, all he felt was confusion and a sense of betrayal. He'd been honest, while everyone else was lying, or so it seemed right now. His head throbbed, and it was difficult to breathe. All he wanted to do was run, but he couldn't move an inch. He couldn't turn off his feelings for her like a faucet. It still dripped through his heart.

"So why are you still pointing a gun at me?" Jasper finally caught his breath when Roman lowered his weapon.

"Because, like I said, I know what is going on even before it happens. Maddy, my lovely

215

matchmaking wife, thinks you two are a match made in heaven, but right now, you both are living a nightmare. You both feel lost and not sure you'll ever trust each other again, and you're wondering whether or not anything between you was real. When you both calm down, you might remember that, at this point in time, with a gun to your heads, you were both willing to die for each other." Roman put his gun away and kissed the top of Maddy's head. "Just like we would. If that isn't love, nothing is. Now, Jasper you close up the back door, and Jackie, you come with us. I think you both need time apart to process everything."

Jackie never looked his way. Jasper turned and left without acknowledging her, either. His heart had been pierced, and there was nothing left to do right now but go somewhere and lick his wounds. Now was not the time to talk things out. Roman was right. The more space between them right now, the better.

Nearing the entrance to the tunnel, the panic attack started to fade. He knew what he needed to do. Grabbing his phone, he called Dom and asked for their location. Before Hower left this earth, he'd be giving Jasper the answers they needed and, with any luck, regain some of the faith his boss had lost in him.

***

Jackie

Jackie thought that when the man responsible for

her parent's death was dealt with, she'd feel something. Triumph, relief, accomplishment, but all that surged through her right now was emptiness. She was numb.

What to do now? An hour from now? Tomorrow?

It was all up in the air.

After Jasper left, they'd gone to Madison's office. Roman and Maddy spent a good hour counseling her through what had happened and what would happen. What to say if police questioned her about Hower. What to do about work—they didn't want her to leave. What to do if she decided to go—she wouldn't be allowed to come back. Despite the promise to her father, once she was out, she wouldn't get back in. Any contact or help from the Caponellis would end. Forever.

When it was time to go home, she couldn't wait to get there. Walking into the apartment, she felt like a zombie. Her purse, her keys, her phone, everything just fell where it landed. She barely remembered stripping off her clothes and stepping into the shower until the cold water stunned her awake. Jackie screamed as her tears mingled with the water dripping down her face. She never needed her mother more than now, and that just caused the waterworks to flow even harder.

It was a lot to take in. Not to mention she'd caused Andrew Hower's death. A living, breathing person was now dead because of her. That was the hardest thing to deal with. She'd not actually done the deed, but by lying and leading him there to be killed, she had as much blood on her hands as Arlo and Dominic. Her relationship with Roman and Madison seemed fragile, but they didn't seem to think anything of it. Her boss still expected her to show up for work on Monday. But could she? Would it be best to just pack the car and leave town? Where would she go, and what would she do? Life right now was a crossroad, and it was hard to know which direction to turn.

A rattling noise brought her back from the brink, and she realized it was her teeth chattering. She trembled so badly, it took several attempts to turn off the water. Grabbing a towel, she dried off and slipped on a fluffy robe. Still cold, Jackie went to the kitchen, grabbed a bottle of whiskey, and started a fire in the fireplace.

A half hour later, the fire roared, and half the bottle was gone. Jackie rocked while staring into the flames. Nothing helped. Nothing made her feel better. It was at if she'd died on the inside, but the outside just didn't know it yet.

In the brief time she'd been in Genoa, the place had become home. A bigger city held zero interest for her now. She liked it here. Being a reporter held zero interest for her, but she liked working at the winery and was excited to see the business grow. Then, there was Jasper. She loved him. As much as she had fought it, he'd won her heart.

Jasper.

She took another swig from the bottle and set it on the floor. Where was he? Jackie stood and paced the room like a caged-in cat. So tied up in her own mess, she'd not considered how much this had affected him. The man must be a turmoil. He loved his life with the family, and she'd made him look bad.

Dishonored.

Guilt spiked when she realized she had no idea where he was, but going to his house right now just didn't seem like the right idea either. Jackie needed time to think things, though, and it was a good bet he did also. Rising slowly, she returned to the kitchen, carefully holding on to chairs and tables along the way. She wasn't used to heavy drinking, and too much booze had made the room sway. Spying her phone on the floor, Jackie carefully reached for it. Hitting the start-up button several times, she realized it was clearly dead. Counting four deep breaths, she found the cord and plugged it in. Maybe it was a good thing it wasn't charged. Right now, she didn't even know where to start, and she was in no condition to form complete sentences.

The clock on the wall said midnight. Where had the time gone? Fighting back a yawn, physical and mental exhaustion overtook her, and Jackie finally fell into bed.

***

Jasper

Never had he wanted to skin a person alive, piece by piece, but right now, Andrew Hower was at the top of that list. Arlo and Dominic didn't appreciate him making them wait to get rid of the guy, but he'd insisted. The urge to do something was overpowering. Ever since things had unfolded at the winery, it'd been hard to process what the hell had gone down. Just driving out of town helped ease the throbbing headache that had formed.

The Restful Arms was anything but. It was a run-down motel that both the MC and mob used for things they'd like to keep under the radar of the local law enforcement. However, once the staff discovered the demise of Hower, they'd have no choice but to call the police.

They were waiting for him in room number thirteen.

"What took you so long?" Dom grumbled as Jasper entered the room. "Stephanie's been waiting. She wants to go out to eat."

"Whipped." Jasper couldn't believe the change in the man since he'd met his true love. The guy had always preferred to be alone, so going out to eat in a restaurant was something new to the man who was uncomfortable around people. Steph had healed the man from the inside out. It was true love, and that just threw more salt on the cuts to his heart he was experiencing right now. "Has he said anything?"

Arlo stepped to his side. "The usual shit. *Help me. I didn't do it. I can get you money.*"

"Nothing about the Bratva or the Smiths." His friend just shook his head. "Did you bring what I asked?"

"Yeah, but this is going rogue." He nodded toward the man tied to a chair. Hower was pale, and from his lack of fight, he had clearly accepted his fate. "Roman said to kill him, not interrogate him. We can't leave any marks. It has to look like a suicide."

"It will. Connie got the insurance money, so they didn't suspect anything there." Jasper now stood in front of the man who'd turned Jackie's world upside down. "Give me the needle." He held out his hand, and Arlo gave him the syringe. It was Amobarbital, which they used to get people to talk. It wasn't actually a truth serum, but it did cause the person's central nervous system to slow down, and they would have a hard time coming up with a fake answer. Even if he couldn't get his girl back, he would prove his worth to his boss.

"A needle pick will leave a mark." Dom moved to stand behind Andrew. "But we're going to hang 'em, so just poke him where the rope will hit. Hold him, and I'll do it." That caused the man to squirm and come to life.

Jasper and Arlo held Hower motionless while Dom inserted the needle in the correct spot, and they waited. The drug made him drowsy but not enough to not answer questions. For the next hour, Jasper asked question after question and recorded it all on his phone. It was risky to do that, but it was important for Roman to hear it word for word. The man revealed the full details of what had happened to Jackie's parents and the names of the men who had murdered them.

It was when they asked him why he had gotten involved with the Bratva that things really got interesting. Andrew hadn't always been a willing accomplice. He was over his head in debt and had agreed to help in return for a payoff. Once he was on the payroll, the man got addicted to the money and the other benefits of working for the Russian mob. The high-end hookers and access to their clubs were just a few of those benefits. The guy gave up the addresses of some of the clubs and major hangouts. He also mentioned that they'd been responsible for some of the hits on Caponelli and Rinaldi businesses.

"What are they planning to hit next?" They didn't have much time left. It was getting late, and the motel would get busy with people paying by the hour. Also, Hower had broken out in a sweat, his skin was clammy, and it looked like he might be going into cardiac arrest. The guy had been under extreme stress for several hours.

"The daughter," he mumbled, and Jasper shook the man awake.

"The daughter? What daughter?" Jasper asked again. "Whose daughter?"

His mind raced as he counted in his head the names of single women in the Caponelli and Rinaldi families who might be the focus of the Bratva. It was anyone's guess who they'd go after, but everyone needed to be extra vigilant.

Andrew jerked as the impending heart attack kicked in, and in a matter of seconds, his head rolled to the side.

"Son of a bitch. Untie him." They loosened the ties that bound him, and Hower collapsed onto the floor in a thud. He was still breathing but not long for the world.

"Well, this makes it easier. We don't have to hang him now and the needle gauge was small enough it didn't show at all." Dom glanced at his watch. "I just got a text from the tech guys saying that everything has been uploaded to his computer and phone. They said to just leave the laptop up and running. Can you finish up? I got to go."

"If everything is swept and clean. Go." Arlo groaned, and his eyes met Jasper's. At least Dom's love life was on the right track, even if theirs weren't.

Dom hustled out, and his van could be heard turning on the crushed rock as he spun out.

"I guess that means you're driving me home." Arlo checked the man for a pulse. "He's dead, but we'd better stay another ten minutes, just to make sure."

"Yeah, sure." Jasper checked his phone for messages, but there were none.

Chapter Twenty-Three

Jasper

The sun was already up when Jasper finally drove into the driveway to his place. What a long fuckin' night. Turning off the car, he checked his phone for the hundredth time. If Jackie cared as much as she said, why hadn't she called? And did he even want her to? After leaving the motel, Arlo and he had driven to Roman's house to play the recording. At least Jasper felt redeemed in Roman's eyes. The man said he knew that Jasper would do what needed to be done and that Jasper was loyal to him. Arlo and Dom had been given instructions to interrogate the guy, if Jasper hadn't beat them to it. He'd played right into their hands again.

The Caponellis and Rinaldis were taking extra precautions to protect their wives and the daughters of everyone in the family. Arlo hadn't said a word, but you could tell he was concerned about Layla. If anyone was a target, she'd be the biggest. With Madison out of town and married to Roman, Layla was the remaining daughter of Bruno Rinaldi in Chicago. The closest dot on their radar.

After business was taken care of, Arlo left, while Jasper stayed to ask about Jackie and where he stood with the family. Again, Roman stressed that he should have been more careful about pursuing the reluctant redhead, but that all was forgiven. She'd be welcomed into the family with open arms, if Jackie wished to stay. Oh God, how he wished she would. Even if there was no future for them, he wanted her to be safe.

Entering stalker mode, he drove past her place. Her car was parked in its usual spot, and nothing seemed out of the ordinary. Finally, Jasper dragged himself out of the vehicle and into his home, where he collapsed onto the couch. There was no way he would sleep in his bed with the scent of her perfume on the pillows. It hurt way too much. He should have hated her, but he didn't. He should have wanted her to leave, but he didn't. He should have gone after someone, but he wouldn't.

In the past few hours, he'd gone through all the stages of grief, only this wasn't a death, but the possible end of relationship. Her betrayal had shocked him beyond belief. It had come out of left field and nailed him with a right hook. She had her reasons for keeping quiet, but she should have trusted him, and that hurt most of all. It's human nature to want to get back at those who harmed you. Was he angry? That was an understatement, but then, he remembered what else she had done.

Jackie had stepped in front of a loaded gun pointed at his chest. She'd accepted death to save his life. How could he say that wasn't love? How could he ever let her go? Groaning, he rolled over and reached for his phone. He'd always regret it if they didn't see this through.

Jasper checked the time on his phone. It was too early to call. She may still have been sleeping. Being overly tired and overly emotional was never a good time to talk. So he sent a text.

Jasper: *We need to talk. 7 tonight at the Pier. Please be there.*

He hit SEND and closed his eyes.

***

Jackie

Her mouth was dry, and her head throbbed like a bitch. Yawning, she rolled to the side and closed her eyes. The sun was up and shinning right through the window. Glancing at her alarm clock, she'd clearly overslept. Reliving what had happened in the last twenty-four hours, she hugged her pillow tighter. Andrew Hower was dead, and her relationship with Jasper was on life support.

Dragging her feet, she headed to the bathroom to freshen up for the day. After a warm bath, yoga pants and a t-shirt were her choice for the day until she knew what came next. Coffee. That was what came next. It briefly crossed her mind to go to the Java Shop, but right now, she didn't feel like talking to anyone. Making her own would have to do.

Jackie spied her phone on the counter where she'd left it late last night to charge. She was afraid to check and find no messages. That was just too much to handle right now. What was needed was some caffeine first.

It was a good thirty minutes later before she gained the nerve to start up the phone. There were several messages, in fact, so she started at the bottom.

There was one from Stephanie, asking if she'd be interested in a girl's trip and bachelorette weekend. It was a group message that also included Valentina and Madison. Jackie was officially included in the mob wives/girls club. Having never been a part of anything like that, she yearned to have close friends to do things with. There were a few reward texts from local businesses. A free cookie with purchase of coffee at the Java shop. Maybe she'd go there, after all. And a free car wash with gas fill-up at the Kwik Trip. The next was from Maddy. She no longer thought of her as Madison, but Maddy, as her friends and family called her.

Madison: I'm worried about you. Let me know how you are, and I expect to see you at work Monday.

Her heart sank that there were no texts from the person she really wanted to hear from. Jackie placed it back on the counter, only to have it vibrate to life. It was Jasper.

Finally!!

The message was brief and to the point, but it

said what she wanted to hear. He wanted to work things out. Well, that's what she hoped it meant.

But could they?

Jasper would have trust issues, and she had a lot to work through as well.

The rest of the day dragged at a snail's pace. Minute by agonizing minute. Even if things didn't work out between her and Jasper, she'd already made the decision to stay. Genoa was home now, and there was no place she'd rather be.

Jackie curled her hair and put on some light makeup. Deciding what to wear was the hard part, but she finally settled on capris, a sleeveless top, and sandals. Standing in front of the mirror one more time before going out the door, Jackie added the infinity earrings, bracelets, and necklace.

It seemed like so much had happened since he had given her that first gift. What was Jasper feeling right now? Would he be angry? He had every reason to be, but it had never been her intention to get him tangled up in this mess. She'd turned him down numerous times, but in the end, he'd won her over. The next few hours would decide her future— *their* future. Anxiety had gotten the best of her, so she decided to get outside again and take a walk before leaving. Wringing her hands, it was the best stress relief she could come up with. Jackie grabbed her phone and keys and went outside.

There was a small wooded park near her building, and that'd be just the trick to calm her nerves and get some much-needed fresh air. All she wanted for the next half hour was a little alone time with nature. Jackie took the path next to the lake. It was basically a hiking path that stopped at different spots in the woods. In the middle was a small park with a few picnic tables and benches. There was also a small parking lot that seem to attract lovers late at night. From what she had heard, anyway. With any luck, it would be too early in the day for that.

It was a good ten-minute walk before she'd get there. Rounding the bend, she spied a white van in one of the parking spots. What was Dominic doing here? Was he checking up on her? Jackie strode alongside the vehicle. Hopefully, the man hadn't had to pick up a body here. The side door was open.

"Dominic?" She poked her head inside, but it was empty.

Thud.

She fell forward onto the hard floor of the van. Her elbows burned as they skidded across the rough surface. Jackie rolled over and rubbed the back of her head. She saw stars. What the hell? Before she knew it, someone shoved her legs in the van and slammed the door shut.

Jackie fought to keep her eyes open. Had Roman changed his mind and decided to get rid of her after all? Not having seen the inside of Dom's van, she couldn't be positive this was it. There was a gate separating the driver and the back. Struggling to sit as the vehicle started up and drove out of the park, the man behind the wheel came into focus. It wasn't Dom. It wasn't anyone she'd ever see before.

"What's going on?" She collapsed back onto the floor. The stranger had hit her over the head. Right now, she should be in panic mode, but the pain was too much to register anything else. It was a concussion, for sure, maybe even a skull fracture.

"Who are you?" The pain caused her to roll up into the fetal position, but she still had a little fight left in her.

"Don't worry, honey." The man in the front seat finally spoke. "Before the night is through, you'll know me really well." His laugh was the last thing she heard before everything went black.

***

Jasper

Jasper was early to the Pier. He didn't want to miss Jackie and was too nervous to sit and wait at his place.

"Can I get you a drink, sweetie?" The waitress stood a little too close. At first, he didn't recognize her, or even care, but it was a good chance they'd shared a drink somewhere or sometime. Her name was Lacy, Tracy, Stacy, or something like that.

"Just a water for now. I'm waiting for someone." He glanced at his phone again.

"Lucky lady." The woman walked away with an exaggerated saunter.

Thirty minutes later, he was still nursing a glass of water and ready to bite off the head of anyone who came in the door and wasn't the one he was waiting for. He glared at the wall clock for the hundredth time. Well, he was done. Jackie wasn't coming. If she was anything, it was punctual. The woman was usually early for everything. Cursing, he got up and threw a few bills on the table before marching out the door to his vehicle. Maybe he'd head to Roman's and punch some bags. The need to hit something was top on his list. Anything to distract him from the emptiness in his chest.

The phone in his pocket vibrated, and hope rose again.

"Jackie?" He didn't bother to look at the scene and kept walking.

"No, this is Christian." The deep voice on the other end wasn't familiar.

"Who?"

"Sorry, this is Christian. I'm one of the tech guys. I work for Roman."

Jasper stopped. He'd texted back and forth with the tech guys many times, but this was the first time he'd ever spoken with one. "Yeah, what's up?" This had him on alert, and he scanned the area for anything unusual.

"One of my duties is to monitor the trackers for abnormal activities."

Jasper took a deep breath. The guy even talked like a techy. "And?"

"The tracker on Miss Smith's necklace got my attention."

It got Jasper's as well, and he gripped the phone tighter. "What do you mean?"

"It was in one spot, with her phone, but now the one on the necklace is leaving town."

"Wait. What?" Leaving town? "Maybe she just left her phone at home and went for a drive."

"No. It's our belief that's she's been taken."

Jasper collapsed against this side of his SUV.

"What the hell do you mean, taken?" His vision blurred.

"She walked to a wooded area near her home. The phone stayed there, but the tracker on her necklace is still mobile. I searched local camera footage, and it appears she's in a white van." White van?

"Is she with Dom?" This made no sense at all.

"No, but he and Arlo are on their way to get you and should be arriving in about thirty seconds." Jasper turned toward the street and could see Arlo hauling ass his direction. "I have Roman standing by as well."

"I don't get it." Fear like he'd never experience crept down his spine. "Is it the Bratva?" He said a silent prayer for that not to be true. Maybe she was just with a friend, but she didn't hang out with anyone else, and why was the phone left behind?

Arlo's SUV skidded to a stop, and he yelled for Jasper to get in. He jumped in the back and had barely closed the door before they took off.

"No." Christian was brief and to the point.

"Then who is she with?" Jasper still couldn't wrap his brain around what was happening.

Dominic turned his way but didn't say anything, a grim look on his face. Finally, Christian spoke up. "We checked the plates. They belong to Alexander Dubnikov."

Jasper's chin dropped to his chest.

No. No. No.

Chapter Twenty-Four

Jackie

Her mouth was dry, and her head throbbed like a mother. She couldn't move, and it took all the effort she had just to open her eyes. Focusing was another struggle. The room was not familiar. The fact that she was strapped to a table was frightening. Jolted awake, Jackie fought the straps that bound her, but it was no use. They were heavy duty, and even a knife would be useless on them.

Had she hit her head and was hallucinating? Had she been double-crossed by the Caponellis or taken by the Bratva? She was supposed to meet Jasper. Where was he? Did he even care or know she was gone?

"Finally. You're awake." A man from the van strolled into the room with a coffee cup in hand. He was relaxed and totally at ease with having a woman tied to a table in what could only be a dining room. A kitchen was visible through the open doorway.

"Where am I, and who are you?" Even talking seemed to take more effort than it should.

"Name's Alexander, and I'm your worst nightmare." He smiled and placed a hand on the table.

"What do you mean?" Fight or flight instinct kicked in, but since she couldn't do either, a chill swept through her body.

"I had so much fun with the last woman I took. I wanted to do it again." The man talked as if holding someone against their will was the same as playing a video game or taking an amusement ride.

"What do you mean, the last woman?" Jackie tried kicking her feet, but they barely moved.

"The girl they found along the road." Alexander took a sip of coffee and leaned back against the wall. "It was on all the news. I'm sure you saw it. Nothing too exciting ever happens in the little town."

"Ah, who is she?"

"My brother's favorite whore. I wanted to get his attention, and now that I have you," he put his hand on her knee, "I have the Caponellis attention, also."

"Why would they care about me? I'm not a Caponelli." She had to keep him talking. Someone had to be coming for her or have noticed she was missing.

"It's too hard to get to Roman's wife or sister, but I watched you with them a few times, so you must be close to the family." He had a slight slur and a Russian accent.

"I just work for them. Nothing else."

Alexander shrugged his shoulders. "A minor

matter. They'll get the message when I throw your body on their front lawn."

"Why would you do that?"

Oh God. Oh God.

She was in the hands of a lunatic. A deranged freak who look like any normal guy who walked the streets. He could have been at the coffee shop or grocery store, and no one would have viewed him as anything out of the normal. Average height and build, short blondish hair, bright blue eyes, and dressed in jeans and a t-shirt.

The guy just shrugged. "Why? Because I want to, and I can."

Jackie took a deep breath, then another. The only weapon she had at her disposal was her wits, and being smart would buy her time. It had to be past the time that Jasper was to meet her. He had to know she was missing, but would he think she just stood him up? She briefly closed her eyes and said a quick prayer.

"You said you wanted to get your brother's attention. Why?" Jackie pulled questions out of the air. Anything to keep him talking instead of doing.

"I'm the oldest, yet he has all the power. Fedor's the one everyone listens to, but once I show what I can do, everyone will be following me, not him." Alexander circled the table. "Do you know what it's like to always be in someone's shadow when you are the first born?"

She swallowed and shook her head.

"It's torture." His eyes jerked back and forth. The guy was high on something or just plain insane. He brushed her hair away from her face. "You're so pretty."

"Is that why I'm here? You thought I was pretty?" This was so messed up. Tears formed at the corners of her eyes, and his face brightened.

"No, that was just a bonus." He placed a cold hand on her bare arm. "You, my dear, were just the easiest target I could get." Alexander dropped his hand and stepped back. "Now, let the fun begin."

"What do you mean?" As hard as she tried to fight it, hysteria filled her veins. Her chest was ready to burst as she gasped for a breath. "Can't we just talk some more?"

"No. I'm done talking. Time to play."

***

Jasper

Christian was on speaker phone and giving coordinates according to the tracker on Jackie's necklace. Hopefully, it was still around her neck. They'd sent one of the other tech guys to the park to retrieve her phone and look for any other clues. Her apartment keys had been found near the dropped cell.

His anxiety level was at a record high. So much for being calm and cool. He was a fucking mess. Thankfully, Arlo was at the wheel, and Dominic had taken over, calling the shots. The man was good at this and not running on emotion. It'd be a different scenario if it were Stephanie who was missing, but then, Jasper would take over. They were both like brothers to him and never more than right now.

"Has the location changed?" Dominic asked. It was a house out in the country that hadn't been lived in for years.

"No. The subject has not moved in the last twenty minutes."

The subject? They were talking about the woman he loved and wanted to spend the rest of his life with. A sharp pain pierced his chest just imaging the fear she must be feeling. Twenty minutes was a long time when you were in the hands of a crazy fucking bastard.

"Give us the layout of the property," Arlo said. They were only a few miles away, but going in guns a-blazing was never a good idea. In two seconds flat, everyone had a beep on their phones and a detailed map and image of the house Christian gave as Jackie's location.

Dominic spoke first. "I say go up and around. We park behind this section of woods and move from there." Arlo grunted, and Jasper drew his gun.

It'd been the longest five minutes of his life, but they finally arrived at the location amongst the trees from where they'd strike. Roman had dispatched a couple of cars for backup, and they were already parked out of sight near the end of the driveway of the farm house they'd soon be breaching.

Adrenaline spiked through his veins as he got out of the car. Jasper took several deep breaths and stepped into mob mode. He brushed aside emotion and became all business. It was the only way to be and the best way to save her—to be a cold-hearted killer and save the one he wanted to spend his life with.

They quietly pressed the doors shut. Phones were put on mute as Arlo told Christian their next steps. Each man wired themselves up for sound and placed in an earpiece. One of the crew around front had dispatched a drone so Roman could monitor the operation. His boss would use it for training later. What to do, or not do, in this case. They were all connected now and could hear anything that happened.

As they approached the edge of the tree line, they studied the layout again. It was an older home with an attached garage. The bastard had probably driven his van into the garage and entered that way.

Dom spoke up. "Any movement visible inside?"

"Some in the front, so you should be good going in around the back. We've got visual of only one man so far," Christian responded.

The men out on the road gave an all clear. They were ready to roll.

"Okay, Dom and I will take the flank, and you go in the front," Arlo instructed, and Jasper nodded. They'd given him the lead roll with them as backup. He'd have fought it if it were any other way. Dom tossed some sunglasses, a trucker hat, and a hoodie his way on the off chance that Alexander might know who he was. "Ring the doorbell, and say your car stopped and your cell is dead. Just keep your head to the side so he can't see the earpiece." Jasper traded his suitcoat for the disguise.

"Yeah, I know the drill." He'd done it many times, but never had it been this important. Jasper both prayed that she was in there and hoped that she wasn't.

They sneaked up to the house with the drone in place. Christian would give a shout out if anyone was seen near a window.

With Arlo and Dom in place, Jasper reluctantly holstered his gun. If the guy caught a peek of that, there was no way he'd open up. Running his fingers through his hair, Jasper made the sign of the cross, pulled the hat down low, and knocked on the front door. Footsteps sounded from inside as they neared, but no one showed.

He knocked again before yelling, "Hello. Anyone home?" Jasper could feel the man's presence on the other side of the door. "My car broke down, and my phone is dead. Can you call someone for me?"

"Subject is by the front door, and I have a visual on Jackie," Arlo's voice sounded in his ear. "Go in on two. One. Two." Glass windows shattered on two sides of the house as he and Dom broke in. Jasper kicked in the door, taking down the man behind it. Jasper was on him in an instant, smashing his face over and over with his fist. He was in a rage as blood spattered the wall and floor around them.

"Stop." Arlo grabbed Jasper from behind and pulled him off. "I'll take care of this piece of shit. You go to her." He nodded toward the hallway before giving the all clear over the radio.

Jasper hurried to the door at the end of the hall, both eager and afraid of what he might find. What he saw would haunt him forever. Jackie lay tied to a table. Dominic stood beside her with a knife trying to cut her loose. Black lines had formed on her face where tears and mascara had mixed together. Her eyes met his, and he rushed to her side as Dom was finally able to get the first strap loose.

"Jackie, my angel." He crushed her to his chest before putting her at arm's length to check her over. "Are you hurt? Did he do anything to you?" The knot in his stomach finally dissolved when she said that he hadn't.

"Thank God you're here." She cried and enveloped her trembling body in his after Dom cut the final tie. "His name is Alexander. He's the man who tortured that poor girl and was about to do the same to me."

Roman voice sounded over the ear piece. "Everything secure?"

"Yes, sir." Several men gave their location and status.

"Dom, how do you want to resolve this?" Arlo asked while dragging Jackie's kidnapper into the room.

"Put him on the table so I can work on him." No one touched his woman and lived to tell about it. Jasper picked Jackie up and carried her to a nearby chair.

Arlo threw the bloody mess of a man onto the table and gathered the ties to strap him down. Jasper untangled himself from Jackie and stood up. He was going to enjoy this. On his way to the task, Dom stood in his way. "I got this."

"Get out of my way. I get the honor." Jasper was going to skin that man alive.

"There's no honor in doing this in front of her." His friend nodded Jackie's way. "I know how you feel, but I will never forget the look on Stephanie's face when I killed Oscar in front of her. She understands this life, but Jackie isn't from our world. You need to protect her." Leave it to Dominic, the man of few words, to say the ones Jasper needed to hear most. "Go, get out of here. We'll finish up."

The man moaned as Arlo pulled a strap tight, and Jackie could be heard crying. She had a kind heart, too kind to be here. "He's mentally ill. He has to be." She would want the man turned in to the police, but that wouldn't happen. The man would die an agonizing death for what he did to the other woman and for what he intended to do to Jackie.

Arlo's phone vibrated, and he answered it. "Roman wants the fucker alive."

"Oh, hell no." Jasper wasn't having any of it. "Over my dead body."

"He might have information we need about the Bratva. We'll work him over and see what spills out. You take her home."

"Son of a bitch!" Jasper groaned and clenched his fist. It was the right thing to do. She needed more than they did here. "Give me the damn keys." Arlo took them out of his pocket and tossed them his way.

"Thanks, guys." Jasper choked up. It'd been an emotional day. "I owe you."

"We're brothers, even if we aren't blood." Dom and Arlo nodded in agreement.

Jasper returned and knelt in front of a very pale Jackie. "Are you okay to go now? Do you want me to carry you?" Jasper took her hands in his.

"Just get me out of here." She let go of his hands and threw her arms around his neck.

"Where do you want to go?" Jasper said in her ear.

"Anywhere as long as it's with you." Jackie held him tight, and he wasn't letting go.

"Don't worry. I'm never leaving you again."

Chapter Twenty-Five

Two months later

Jackie

There was nothing better than being kissed awake by the one you loved. Jasper nibbled on her ear before dropping his mouth to her neck, then her breasts. They didn't have much time, so their lovemaking this morning would be quick but no less mind-blowing. She'd barely awoken before he was pressed up against her opening, ready to make her his.

A moan escaped her lips as he thrust inside her. The fast pace her man kept was matched only by her own. They'd become so in tune with each other's needs, it didn't take long to reach climax when short on time. Tonight would be different. Jasper was an expert at playing her body like a fine-tuned instrument, and he promised to make up for their fast and furious wake-up call.

Her muscles tightened, and before she knew it,

Jackie was spiraling over a passion-filled cliff. Jasper shuddered and groaned as he followed after. His hands clutched in hers above her head.

"Have I told you today how much I love you?" Jasper ran his fingers through her tousled hair.

"No, I don't believe so." Her cheeks were flushed as she tightened her legs around his, not wanting him to leave her body just yet.

"You're my angel, and I love you more and more every day."

"I love you, too."

Jasper's phone alarm buzzed, and he rested his forehead on hers. "Damn. I guess I'd better get dressed."

"Yes. We can't be late." They had a ceremony to get to.

***

The wedding of Stephanie and Dominic was something out of a bohemian and medieval dream, with the bride looking like a beautiful princess and the groom a handsome prince. They'd both wanted a low-key ceremony out in the woods, but with tensions high and security a priority, both parties agreed that the nuptials would be best if they took place at Roman and Madison's place.

It was a beautiful June day. The sun was shining as the boats buzzed by on the lake. Jackie adjusted her skirt as it lightly ruffled in the breeze. She had a front row seat for the festivities. A lot had happened since her arrival in this town. It was home now, and she couldn't imagine living anywhere else.

Her relationship with Jasper had never been
better or stronger. Her cheeks blushed as he winked
at her from where he stood. He was the best man
today and had never looked more handsome. Both
he and Dom were dressed similarly, which was a
first. Reluctantly, Dom had let Jasper pick out their
clothes for the wedding. They were both dressed in
mustard-colored pants, ivory dress shirts, and brown
suspenders. The groom wore a tie, while Jasper
went without. Dom wore his long hair tied back and
had trimmed his beard short.

They stood near a dark wood awning that was
draped with wild flowers and navy-blue satin, the
accent color of the wedding. There were few people
in attendance as both Stephanie and Dominic didn't
like crowds. Just the men and women who were
close to them. Jackie noticed Arlo standing in the
back, his eyes always searching the distance for
threats but often returning to the young woman with
long dark hair sitting across the aisle from her.
Jackie had finally gotten to meet Layla at the
bachelorette party. As everyone had hinted at, the
guy really did only have eyes for her.

Just thinking about the girls' weekend
surrounded her with a warm, fuzzy feeling. After
her parents' death, Jackie had distanced herself
from friends, and the fun adventures they'd shared
already made her feel like a welcome addition to the
group, something she'd not experienced in a long
time. They didn't do anything fancy, just got
mani/pedis, watched movies, went shopping, and
drank wine in the hot tub of the resort where they'd
stayed. All were memories which she'd treasure for

a long time.

She'd only been gone two days, but it was hard to tell who had missed the other more, Jasper or herself. After they'd saved her from Alexander, Jasper had brought her to the Caponelli compound to see the family doctor. Luckily, she'd only suffered a mild concussion, but he waited on her hand and foot for much longer than was necessary. Alexander, on the other hand, wasn't doing so well. Jasper would only tell her bits and pieces of what had happened to her captor. They'd kept him alive in the hopes of using the guy against his brother. Whether Fedor would want him back or even care what happened to him was anybody's guess.

After she'd been rescued, they had worked through their differences. Jasper accepted the fact that he'd been the unknowing part of their trap to catch Andrew Hower, and she'd accepted the fact that, even though he was the best man she knew, his job often skirted and even broke the law. Jasper moved in with her, and the view of the lake had never been better, now that he was by her side.

The wedding march started, and the guests turned their attention to the house. Madison was the maid of honor. She was a vision in blue walking down the aisle to take her place opposite Jasper. Jackie sent her a wave as Maddy dabbed at tears with a lacy handkerchief.

Everyone stood as Stephanie exited the house on the arm of her father. Her dress had been designed by Maddy, and it couldn't have been more perfect. The ivory lace dress was sleeveless with a deep V in the front. It had a full skirt that became a short train in the rear. A blue satin ribbon wrapped around her waist and tied into a bow right below the V in the back.

Her long blonde hair was a work of art. Delicate wisps of baby's breath and wild flowers were entwined in the curls. Dominic didn't have to say a word; the look on his face said volumes. Her groom loved her to the moon and back. Jackie's gaze shifted to Jasper. The man was focused only on her. He mouthed, "I love you." She clasped her hands in front of her heart and bit back the sigh threatening to escape her lips.

He'd not proposed yet, but they'd talked about marriage. Both agreed they didn't want to take the spotlight away from the two getting hitched today. There was plenty of time for that later. When the bride reached the arch, her father kissed her cheek and placed her hand in Dom's. The ceremony was short, sweet, and so perfect. When the minister said it was time to kiss the bride, there wasn't a dry eye in the crowd. Dominic beamed, and Stephanie gushed with bliss. The groom led his bride down the aisle, and Roman, who sat in the front row, came up to escort the maid of honor, leaving Jasper all by himself.

With a playful glint in his eye, he strode her way and offered the crook of his elbow. "Hey there, Angel. Care to walk down the aisle with me?" It was an offer she couldn't resist.

"I'd love to." She wrapped her fingers around his arm. He briefly covered them with his before dropping a kiss to her cheek. Jasper had never looked more handsome. Was it the suit? The occasion? No, she'd just fallen more and more under his spell every day.

They enjoyed a small catered meal from Firenza in the formal dining room. Again, the bride and groom hated attention, so no dance or reception would be taking place. Stephanie and Dominic did sit at the head of the table, which was usually Roman's spot. He gave up the honor to sit along the side with his emotional wife, who tittered back and forth between laughter and joyful tears.

Everyone took their seats at the large table, and servers filled their glasses with champagne. All except for Maddy, who placed her hand over her flute and asked for ginger ale. Stephanie's gaze met Jackie's when they noticed it at the same time.

Jasper tapped a knife against his glass and stood. "As best man, it is my duty to give a toast, but where do I begin?" He paused and glanced around the room before settling his gaze on the happy couple. "I can't tell you how happy I am for my two friends, Stephanie and Dominic. People always say that, but until you've felt that love for another person yourself," Jasper looked at her and Jackie's heart nearly burst, "you don't really appreciate how wonderful that feeling is." Her eyes watered, and Madison started the waterworks again. "I know Dom didn't like me when we first met, but I somehow won him over with my charm." That brought a chuckle from the other diners. "I'm proud to call him my best friend. I wish you both a long life of happiness and love, and I look forward to being with you guys every step of that journey. *Salut*." Everyone echoed the toast and drank to the couple as Jasper hugged Dom and Steph. "And I expect to be godfather to some babies also," he joked before taking a seat.

"Thank you, Jasper." Stephanie's face flushed, and she focused on Madison. "But from the way someone's acting, I think the family will be having a new addition very soon." All eyes turned Madison's way.

This time, it was Roman who stood up with a glass in his hand. "Since you brought it up..." He offered a hand to his wife and Madison stood beside him. "We were going to wait a bit before announcing, but I'm so proud to share that my beautiful wife is pregnant." Now that explained her boss's odd behavior the last few weeks. Maddy had been concerned about getting pregnant, and here she was already.

Everyone cheered, and the room burst with love and congratulations. Another round of toasts was in motion for the happy couples, and Jasper clasped her hand on the table.

"Thank you everyone." Maddy glowed with happiness. "Jackie, this means I'm going to be relying on you a lot more in the coming months."

"I'm ready and happy to do it." Never before had she been so excited for the future.

"So, do you two have anything to share with the rest of us?" Madison had just put them on the spot, and Jackie's cheeks burned.

"Soon." Jasper spoke up. "Very soon." Again, the room erupted with cheers and good wishes.

When it finally settled down, Arlo hollered, "Are we ever going to eat?" The man was lucky enough to be sitting next to Layla, but it still hadn't improved his temperament. He soon received more razzing from the others at the table.

"Yes." Madison motioned for the servers to start the meal, and Roman held his glass up in a toast.

"To family." He made it a point of meeting the eyes of every person in the room. "Blood and non-blood. New," he motioned to Stephanie, "old, and future." On the word "future," he directed his glass at Jackie. This time, the tears couldn't be held back, and she squeezed Jasper's hand. She'd lost her family, and they would always be special and close to her heart, but now, she'd been blessed with a new one.

After dinner, Roman had chartered a yacht to take everyone for an evening cruise. It was a chance to relax and continue the traditions of the day. The wedding couple cut into their two-tier chocolate cake at the reception but brought more onboard the ship. Madison was the one who always debated on whether or not to have cake at the coffee shop, but this time, she didn't hold back and asked for two pieces.

"Hey, do you want to go up top to sit for a while?" Jasper asked Jackie before biting into the last piece of his dessert.

"Sure. I'd love to." Everyone had settled into their little groups and barely noticed that they were leaving.

The beautiful day had turned into an equally stunning night. It was warm with a slight breeze. People along the shore were also enjoying their time outside, either sitting on the decks or barbecuing.

"My angel, Jackie." Jasper guided her eyes to his with his index finger.

"What?" Her nerves kicked in.

"Life is short, and I don't want to waste a minute of it without you. I love you with all my heart. I promise to be true to you and only you for the rest of my life. Will you do me the honor of becoming my wife?" He dropped to one knee. "Become Mrs. Lencioni?"

Her mouth fell open. Even though they'd talked about it, it was still a shock to hear. They hadn't known each other that long, but it really didn't matter. Her heart pounded in her chest as Jasper reached into his pocket and pulled out a little red box. She melted even more when he opened it and placed it on her finger. It featured two large diamonds in the middle of an infinity shape.

"Since it's already on her finger, I hope your answer is yes?" Never had she seen the overly cocky Jasper appear nervous, but he was a little pale. The urge to tease him a bit briefly crossed her mind, but she was too eager to give her answer.

She cupped his jaw in her palm. "I love you so much, Jasper. For infinity and beyond, you have my heart."

"Is that a yes?" He appeared even more anxious.

Jackie nodded as tears threatened her eyes. "Of course, it's a yes. Yes. Yes. Yes."

Barely was the last word out of her mouth before his lips were on hers. He tasted like a chocolate cake, champagne, and happily ever after. Loud booms exploded in the background, and they reluctantly broke apart as fireworks lit up the sky over Lake Genoa. It was the end of an absolutely amazing day with an equally amazing man. He'd turned her empty world upside down and overflowed it with love. For today, for tomorrow, and for infinity.

The End

About the Author

Ginger Ring is an award-winning author with a weakness for cheese, dark chocolate, and the Green Bay Packers. She loves reading, watching great movies, and has a quirky sense of humor. Publishing a book has been a lifelong dream of hers and she is excited to share her romantic stories with you. Her heroines are classy, sassy and in search of love and adventure. When Ginger isn't tracking down old gangster haunts or stopping at historical landmarks, you can find her on the backwaters of the Mississippi River fishing with her husband.

Facebook Writer Page:
https://www.facebook.com/romancewritergingerring

Twitter:
https://twitter.com/GingerRings

Webpage & Blog:
http://gingerring.com/

Amazon Author Page:
http://amzn.to/1fslijd

Pinterest:
http://www.pinterest.com/Gingernovel/

Instagram:
https://www.instagram.com/ringginger/

Note From the Author...

I love to write stories that take place in my home state of Wisconsin. The inspiration for the setting of this story is the beautiful tourist town of Lake Geneva. I changed the name to Genoa for the story but forgot that there is a real town called Genoa in Wisconsin. Both are beautiful places to see, so if you ever travel to Wisconsin, make sure to visit both.

There really is a Wollersheim Winery, and it's located in the beautiful community of Prairie Du Sac. I tried to do my best in remembering all the details I learned on my wine tour there, but you really need to see the place yourself. They also make some truly wonderful wine.

I hope you enjoyed this Caponelli family story, as there is more to come.

Join our Reader Group on Facebook and don't miss out on meeting our authors and entering epic giveaways!

Limitless Reading

Where reading a book
is your first step to becoming
limitless...

LIMITLESS ▽ PUBLISHING *Reader Group*

Join today! *"Where reading a book is your first step to becoming limitless..."*

https://www.facebook.com/groups/Limitle ssReading/